Praise for Susan Hatler's Work

"A Fantastic Start to a Fun New Series!"
— *Getting Your Read On*

"Ms. Hatler has a way of writing witty dialogue that makes you laugh-out-loud throughout her stories."
— *Night Owl Reviews*

"I am a huge fan of Susan Hatler!!! I have yet to read a book I did not absolutely love!"
— *Tifferz Book Reviewz*

"Hatler is my go-to girl for a sizzling clean romance with swoon-worthy kisses!"
— *Books Are Sanity!!!*

"Susan Hatler's books make me laugh out loud while also touching my heart."
— *Virna DePaul, New York Times & USA Today Bestselling Author*

Titles by Susan Hatler

Kissed by the Bay Series
Every Little Kiss
The Perfect Kiss
Just One Kiss
The Sweetest Kiss
All About That Kiss

Better Date than Never Series
Love at First Date
Truth or Date
My Last Blind Date
Save the Date
A Twist of Date
License to Date
Driven to Date
Up to Date
Déjà Date
Date and Dash

Treasured Dreams Series
An Unexpected Date
An Unexpected Kiss
An Unexpected Love
An Unexpected Proposal
An Unexpected Wedding
An Unexpected Joy
An Unexpected Baby

Young Adult Novels
Shaken
See Me
The Crush Dilemma

Every Little Kiss

(Kissed by the Bay, #1)

Susan Hatler

Every Little Kiss
Copyright © 2015 by Susan Hatler

ISBN-13: 978-1518684425
ISBN-10: 1518684424

Cover Design by Elaina Lee, For The Muse Design
www.forthemusedesign.com

Chapter One

As I drove down California's scenic coastal Highway 1, a sign indicated I would hit my hometown of Blue Moon Bay in two miles and I had to fight the urge not to slam on the brakes, do a fast U-turn, and head back home to Sacramento. Although Blue Moon Bay used to be my home, I hadn't been there since the day I'd left after high school graduation, and I hadn't planned to come back now. I'd tucked that part of my life away and didn't like to think about it—*ever*.

But my grandma's lawyer had called yesterday, informing me that she'd passed away and had left me controlling interest in her quaint and quirky Inn at Blue Moon Bay. The shocking news of her death had sucked the air out of my chest and left me shaky and weak, reaching out to grab hold of the kitchen counter to keep from spilling to the floor.

How could my grandma be gone? I'd just seen her in Napa last month when we'd celebrated her seventy-second birthday and she'd seemed fine. There hadn't been one sign that she'd soon drop dead from a heart attack in the middle of her weekly pinochle game.

As I was reeling in my grief, the lawyer proceeded to tell me that the will stated my brother, Brian, and I couldn't keep the inn. Grandma had apparently added an odd requirement to her will: I had to sell the inn "in person" after running it with my brother for one last month. If I failed to follow those conditions then the inn would be donated to charity and both Brian and I would get nothing.

Even if I'd been willing to give up my inheritance—I wasn't a millionaire or anything but my real estate business was booming—I certainly wouldn't mess things up for my brother, and my grandma would've known that. She obviously had some kind of plan up her sleeve, by forcing my return. Not fair, Grandma. Not fair.

She should've just left the inn to Brian, since he was the one who'd stayed with her after I left nine years ago. Last night, I'd talked on the phone with my brother, whose voice sounded hoarse with grief. He'd also sounded upset about our grandma's decision but mostly the explanation she'd left for him in a letter: she wanted us to sell the inn because I'd have no interest in running it (true enough), and while Brian would, she felt it was time he found his own path (he disagreed). Grandma seemed as pushy from the grave as she had been in life.

I gripped the steering wheel, and my eyes watered. This was the last time my grandma would be bossing us around. She'd believed in hard work and doing your chores, and hadn't been an emotional person in the slightest. But I'd always known she loved us, even if she hadn't shown it in an outwardly way. It was hard to believe I'd never see her again.

As I continued down the highway toward the inn and my brother, hot tears slipped down my cheeks and I swiped them away. To help clear my emotions, I cracked the window of my white Mercedes SUV and breathed in the salty sea air—a hint of blooming flowers wafting in as well.

Along with the familiar scent, painful memories from my past overtook me and I shuddered. I'd been enjoying the city life in Sacramento, purposely not looking back to my time in Blue Moon Bay. Grandma hadn't wanted a memorial service and she'd known I never wanted to come back here again. But she'd mandated that I sell the inn "in person" anyway. Stubborn woman.

My lips twitched as I imagined the crinkle that would be between my grandma's brows and the stern look she'd be giving me if she were here right now. She'd tell me to stop complaining and do what must be done. End of story. Then I'd do what I wanted, anyway. Like grandma, like granddaughter. I'd apparently inherited her "stubborn" gene. Wow, I really missed her.

I cruised down the gray ribbon of highway by the coastline, and spotted the cheery sign welcoming me to Blue Moon Bay. My throat tightened. Nine years. Had it really been that long? I was barely eighteen when I'd left to start a new life in Sacramento, working as a receptionist in a real estate office to support myself through college. I'd worked hard, too, just like my grandma had taught me, and moved my way up the real estate ladder in record time.

Pushing everything else aside, I'd focused on work and it had paid off big time.

Now, at twenty-seven, I was known by everyone in Sacramento as Wendy Watts, the Queen of Realtors. I had a great income and my Realtor photo was plastered on billboards across the city. In the photo, I'd pasted on a smile and worked to communicate confidence and intelligence in my emerald green eyes . . . a confidence I didn't always feel. But I needed people to know I was serious about getting them the home of their dreams, which I did—time after time. And I would continue to do so.

Just as soon as I got back from Blue Moon Bay, anyway. . . .

The inn was on the southernmost tip of the bay, so I would have to cross through the entire town to get there. I wasn't sure I was ready to drive through my past just yet, but that's where the road was taking me. I drove around a bend and the scattering of trees broke apart, revealing dazzling blue waves rolling onto a sandy shore that stretched away from tufts of grass and waving wildflowers whose colorful faces turned up toward the sun.

Seeing the ocean took my breath away and little spangles of sunlight bounced off the water in coin-shaped flashes of gold. The sand glimmered from the shore. I knew from experience that sand would be chilly and crumbly under my bare feet.

As I approached the northern edge of town the white lighthouse came into view, jetting up against the hazy blue sky, black granite rocks strewn around its large base.

A smile played on my lips as I remembered my first kiss right there at the lighthouse one cool summer evening in seventh grade. Benny Lee, a local boy who I'd liked for all of a week. I wondered how life had turned out for him. He was all freckly and big toothed back then, but he'd shared his bag of homemade popcorn with me before he'd made his move. I smiled as that kiss flashed through my head—he'd pressed his mouth against mine and made an adult moaning noise that had me fighting to hold in laughter.

I'd been the first of my group to be kissed by a boy and my best friends had giggled profusely as I gave them every last detail. Where were Olivia, Megan, and Charlie now? I had no idea. I'd lost touch with everyone except my brother and my grandma.

With a sigh, I tore my eyes away from the lighthouse as my car entered the beginning of town, heading toward the inn and my brother. I passed Over the Moon, the ancient local diner—that building was still standing?—and a rush of images flooded my brain, breaking through the wall I'd spent my life building.

My stomach roiled and my hands went a little shaky at the sight of the diner, so I pulled over to the side of the road, staring back at the diner's peeling paint. I'd eaten my last breakfast with my parents right there at that diner before they'd left—for good. I was eight years old and Brian was ten.

Brian and I had been excited about eating out . . . until Mom and Dad sprang their decision on us. They were leaving and we were to stay with Grandma.

When Brian and I had been growing up, my parents were always nomadic. No place could hold their interest long. They would go wherever the wind blew them . . . Guatemala, Peru, and we'd even lived in a hut in Bolivia for a year. We moved around a lot but when Brian and I became school-aged—my parents had home-schooled us—we'd started complaining about having to leave our friends. So my parents moved to Blue Moon Bay in order to "settle down for the kids," living with my dad's mom at the inn.

For a few months our lives seemed perfect. Brian and I enrolled in the public elementary school, made friends we knew we could keep, and played on the beach at the inn until dusk every day. Then my parents made the decision to move on and leave us behind, crushing our brief sense of stability.

Sitting here now, I could still recall how my heart had broken in two by my parents' news. I'd loved them dearly and I was devastated—utterly destroyed—that they were abandoning us. I crumpled, tears flowing, and begged them not to leave. But Mom and Dad didn't comfort me. They just tried to assure me that we'd be happier living a stable life with Grandma.

Since my brother and I had always been close, I turned to him for comfort, trying to wiggle under his arm. But he kept a distance from me from that moment on. When Mom and Dad started talking about where they were going next, he'd whispered to me, "People can't count on anyone but themselves. You should learn that now."

Those were the words I'd tried to live by.

Taking a deep breath, I pushed that awful morning out of my mind and merged back onto the highway as my thoughts returned to my grandma. After our parents left, she'd become my role model. Brian and I pretty much gave each other the same standoff-ish tough love that she gave us.

I pulled into town. Houses lined either side of the highway. Many were vacation homes, places where people came and stayed for the season before heading back to their regular lives. I once dreamed of owning one of those homes, coming back summer after summer with my own children, but now? Viewing the houses as a Realtor, I saw them for their coastal value only. *Cha-ching.*

On the ocean side, most houses were two-story and sometimes three-story affairs with large porches and sweeping balconies. Every window brought a view of the water or the lighthouse or the small fingers of land that jutted out into the ocean on the north and the south, making the semi-circular shape of Blue Moon Bay (population 20,000). The views alone were worth plenty of cash in California's hot real estate market.

I stopped at a red light downtown, admiring the familiar little streets that trailed off the highway, fancifully paved in cobblestones. Much about Blue Moon Bay remained the same: the familiar seafood restaurants, pretty architecture, and usual coastal decorations. I always loved the mix of colors—blues, greens, yellows, and more—throughout the town, all of them bright and cheery and very Spanish Colonial.

The light turned green and I passed paved streets now, leading to more businesses and the schools. Then the highway took a sharp turn before rolling out on that southernmost finger of land. I had deliberately not looked that way on the drive. The inn sat out there on the bluff, overlooking the ocean and as I turned south, I couldn't avoid seeing it any longer.

The Inn at Blue Moon Bay.

My heart skipped a beat and conflicting feelings washed over me as I stared at the impressive building of this quaint coastal inn, its white exterior tinted the colors of the setting sun and the refracted colors of the ocean. The best and worst times of my life had been here.

I zoomed through the gates—which had never once

been closed in all the time I'd lived there—and down the swooping cobblestone drive toward the grand circular entrance. I parked next to several other luxury cars and turned off the motor.

Looking at the inn, it appeared as if nothing had changed—like Grandma would be on the other side of those doors, sweeping the lobby, or bringing out freshly baked cookies for the guests. But she'd never do those things again.

The back of my eyes burned. Feeling like I was eight years old again, I wanted to cling to my brother for comfort. He'd sounded gruff on the phone, though. Maybe he blamed me as much as Grandma that we had to sell the inn. If so, this was going to be a very awkward month.

Either way, I was back.

****

I stepped out of the SUV and the cool ocean breeze swished through my clothes, whipping my hair back away from my face. I needed to go inside my former home and face my brother. Not easy, given that our grandma had died and left *me* in charge of selling the inn even though I was the one who had left nine years ago. Yeah, this wouldn't be too uncomfortable or anything.

Taking a deep breath, I strode through the front doors and stopped short when I spotted my brother standing behind the welcome desk. He wore a brown short-sleeved button-up shirt that matched his dark hair, which fell across his forehead into his emerald green eyes. I fought the instinctive urge to tell him to get a haircut. But that was my brother. His hair always looked messy, like he'd just gone for a run on the beach. Maybe he had.

Obviously he was deep in thought about something since he didn't seem to notice I'd come in. He wiped at the dark wood, a thoughtful frown on his handsome face, making me wonder if he was thinking about Grandma. A box sat next to him, filled with official-looking papers. Perhaps something to do with the estate?

My stomach knotted. Brian and I had both lost our grandma. We were the only ones in the world who knew what the other was going through. We'd both lost the woman who'd basically raised us. Maybe the pain of our shared loss would be enough to make us close again. Since I'd received the call last night, that was all I wanted. We only had each other now.

As if Brian sensed me, he suddenly lifted his head and met my gaze. His eyes immediately lit up, then his emotion faded as quickly as it had come. He cleared his throat. "Hey, sis." He pushed papers around on the counter, as if trying to appear busy. Then his brows came together. "Or should I say, Wendy Watts, star Realtor to the rich, who is here to sell my home out from under me?"

I flinched at his harsh tone. I'd been about to give him a hug, but so much for thinking we'd comfort and console each other. "Brian, I'm here to see *you*."

"No." He shook his head dismissively, then patted the top of the small stack of papers. "You're only here because Grandma's will forced you to come. This is our ancestral estate, but you probably don't even care that we have to sell the inn. Do you?"

"Selling the inn was Grandma's choice. Not mine," I snapped, feeling immediately defensive. I knew he was hurting, but still. It wasn't fair to blame me when I'd done nothing wrong. Talk about misplaced anger. I leaned back against the counter, and blew out a breath.

"Grandma's lawyer told me she didn't want a service. Is that what you heard, too?"

"Yeah." His voice thickened and he ducked his head, avoiding my gaze. He kicked his foot lightly against the counter in a boyish way. "Didn't surprise me."

"Like Grandma told us, right? *Stop fussing and get on with it.*" I thought my gruff tone was a pretty good impression of her, but my chest tightened and the back of my eyes burned. I swallowed, blinking rapidly. "Oh, Brian. What are we going to do without her?"

"I don't know." He flicked his gaze at me, then turned away and disappeared into the back room.

Had I upset him? I hadn't meant to. Sigh. Guess it was going to be harder than I thought to get us close again. As I set my purse behind the front desk, I heard a door shut in the other room. A moment later Brian returned with two cold bottles of beer and handed one to me. Was he raising a white flag with those drinks?

He lifted his bottle toward mine. "To Grandma."

"I'm sure she'd love us drinking beer to her name." The sarcasm leaked from my voice and I clinked the neck of my bottle to his then took a long, refreshing sip of the hoppy liquid.

Brian leaned back against the counter next to me, his shoulder brushing against mine as he gave me a side-glance. "Why did you never come back here? Really?"

My stomach clenched. This time, instead of remembering my parents abandoning us, my thoughts zeroed in on what cinched my expedient departure after graduation: my high school boyfriend, Ian McBride. He'd been the one person I'd opened up to, and for two years I'd felt safe with him. I *never* imagined he would hurt me. He graduated a year earlier than me and went off to college. They say distance makes the heart grow fonder. For Ian, distance made him fall for someone else and dump me. I'd been devastated, to say the least.

I'd let him get too close. I *never* made that mistake with a man again.

Not like I'd tell my brother that though, so I nudged his elbow. "I have a thriving career in the city and it's hard to get away. My life is in Sacramento. There's even a townhome I want to buy that's going on the market soon."

His features tightened. "I see. You've always had

your priorities."

Ouch. Direct hit. "Look, you don't have to stay in Blue Moon Bay once the inn sells. Grandma felt like you needed to follow your own path, and maybe she was right. We'll split the proceeds from the sale and you'll have the money to do whatever you want with your life." I paused a moment. "Maybe you can come to the city with me."

He took a swig of beer. "No. I'm not a city guy. Blue Moon Bay is my home."

The fact that he'd rejected me without a second's pause hurt. I sipped my beer, and sighed. I'd had enough pain for one day. "I'll go to the car and get my bags. Tomorrow we can evaluate what needs to be done with the inn so we can put it on the market."

His eyes became dark and unreadable. "What needs to be *done?*"

"Well, sure . . ." I cringed under the weight of his gaze. I drained the rest of my drink and set it on the counter with a *clank*. With my brother's bad attitude, I was definitely going to need another beer. Probably several. "We'll need to do a walk-through, determine the condition of the inn, and if it needs any repairs. Plus, we should see if there are any short-term projects we can do to increase the sales price."

"Nothing around here needs changing." He grabbed my empty bottle, left the room again, and came back with fresh beers. "But if you want to knock your socks off going from room to room, then there's no time like the present."

I was bone-tired from the last twenty-four hours, but I could see the challenge in my brother's eyes. He was not going to let this go. Stubborn, just like Grandma. And like me, for that matter. So I would rise to his challenge. "Fine. Let's do it."

I moved from room to room, checking things out, with my brother trailing behind me. The smells and sounds made me feel like I was eight again. I fought to keep the memories of my parents at bay, but it turned out replacing them with memories of Grandma made me sad in an entirely different way—like a punch in the gut that hit me hard.

We strolled through the kitchen, lounge area, and exercise room. "The hardwood floors need to be stripped and redone. The windows need to be cleaned. Fresh paint for the walls," I said, making a mental checklist. "We're also going to have to do something about the closed restaurant on the property. I know Grandma had planned to reopen it at some point, but right now it's an empty building. So, we'll have to stage it or something."

"Apparently you're the boss, since Grandma left you controlling interest over the sale," he said, with a sharp edge to his tone.

"Not my choice," I reminded him. Tears stung my eyes but I blinked them back. Get a grip, girl. I would *not* break down now. I cleared my throat and told myself to handle this process as I would with any other cranky client—simply evaluating real estate for a sale. Nothing emotional about that. "Why don't we take a look at the library next?"

He made a noncommittal noise, but at least he'd stopped giving me the evil eye. Then he strode in ahead of me and gestured around the library. "As you can see, we turned this room into a business center as well."

I gazed around the large room, taking everything in. The library was a shared area with three long sofas and a love seat gathered around a big fireplace. There was a large flat screen TV above the fireplace—a new addition—and a few small desks on the far wall, each with a computer on them. A drop leaf table sat against one wall with a stack of puzzles and board games on it. The opposite wall held massive bookshelves with volumes of books, old and new alike. The detailed carvings on the wood were exquisite.

"The bookshelves are amazing." I stared at them, taking in the unique detailed beauty. "They're obviously custom. Who did Grandma hire to make those?"

"I did them." His tone was casual, humbly dismissing the time and care he must've put into the ornate design, as if his work was no big deal.

"When did you get interested in woodworking?" I turned to him, but he just shrugged in answer. Hmm. I wondered if Grandma had declined to leave Brian the inn because she'd seen his woodworking talent. Maybe *this* was what she felt he was supposed to be pursuing.

"Had to talk Grandma into the big screen," he said, interrupting my thoughts. He raised his beer toward the giant flat-screen TV. "Told her it was time to come into the twenty-first century. We watched some really entertaining shows on that screen. Speaking of . . . are you still dating that guy, Chase?"

"You watched the show?" I placed a hand over my heart, touched that he even knew the name of the bachelor I'd dated on Sacramento's reality TV special, *Romance Revealed.* I'd purchased a starring role on the reality special through a charity auction, but another couple won the grand prize. I had to admit they seemed to be well suited. More than Chase and I had been.

He chuckled. "We watched every single episode. Grandma and I were rooting for you to win the grand prize money even though we thought you were faking interest in that poor shmuck."

"I wasn't faking interest in Chase." I rolled my eyes and took a sip of beer, which was finally starting to hit me a little. Chase was a decent guy and we'd dated a few more times after the show ended a few weeks ago. But there had been no sparks between us. Not even half a spark. "He was nice, but it didn't work out."

"That's too bad," he said, actually sounding like he meant it.

"Thanks." I trudged up the grand staircase, wondering if my brother might be softening a little toward me. Or maybe I was just starting to feel a little woozy from the alcohol. "Are *you* dating anyone special?"

He shook his head. "Nah. Megan and I still hang out sometimes, though."

I shot him a look, nerves creeping up my spine. Did he mean *my* Megan? As in, my old friend from high school? "How, uh, is she?"

He gave me a lopsided grin. "I see what you're thinking. There's nothing going on between us. She's dating some tool from the yacht club. Just make sure to see her while you're in town or I'm the one who will have to hear about it later." He laughed, a soft, musical sound that made this feel almost like old times.

"We'll see," I said, studying him. His attitude seemed so hot and cold that I wasn't sure how to take him. It would be nice to see Megan again, but in addition to putting the inn on the market, I had to stay on top of my business, which meant keeping in constant communication with my assistant who was holding down the fort for me. I glanced up at the ceiling above the staircase and jerked to a halt. "Is that water damage?"

"Minor leak." His tone was casual but his face tightened up, which told me the leak concerned him more than he was going to say. "I've got a tarp over the problem until there's more money in the budget for roof repairs."

"We need to fix that." I pressed a hand to my forehead, hoping that really was a minor problem. Water damage was nothing to mess around with. Throughout the upstairs hallway, I opened doors to peek into the six guest rooms on this wing's floor. Each room had its own tiny bathroom and a view of the beach. "So far, we need the roof repaired, floors refinished, painting, and a deep cleaning. We're going to have quite a busy month."

His forehead creased as he turned for the stairs. "Yeah, then you'll be outta here. Back to your fancy life in the city." He blew out a breath. "Just like after you graduated, I'm sure you'll fly out of here like we all have the plague."

"That's what people do after graduating, Brian. They grow up and leave and make their own way." At the bottom of the stairs, I hurried down the winding hall toward the front counter where I'd left my purse. "It's called becoming independent."

"Yeah, because you can't count on anyone else to take care of you," he quipped, throwing his words from long ago in my face like they were venom.

I turned and faced him. "Aren't *you* the one who taught me that?"

He didn't answer, but his eyes darkened as he stopped in front of the welcome desk. Man, oh, man. What was up with Brian? He and I weren't super close, but he was a nice guy and never lashed out like this. I glanced up at him, but he turned away from me and took a long drink of his beer, finishing it off.

The back of my eyes stung as I waited, unsure if I should get my bags from my car, or wait for him to say something else to hurt me. Then I realized what I should've guessed sooner. He was grieving over our grandma. Our parents hadn't visited much after they moved on, and I'd only heard about them coming to the inn once since I moved to Sacramento. Now that Grandma was gone, all he had was me, and I'd be leaving soon.

Swallowing my pride, I took a small step toward him. "I'm sorry, Brian."

He lifted his head, a confused look on his face. "For what?"

"About Grandma," I said, softly. I watched him turn away from me, press his hands against the counter then drop his chin to his chest. I longed to reach forward and put my arms around him, but I feared he'd brush me off. My feet stayed planted where they were and that tight spot in my chest turned in on itself. "I'm *truly* sorry."

A minute passed in silence. "Me, too," he finally said. Then he lifted his head, turned, and faced me. "Now we're selling my home," he said, his voice raw with emotion.

He sounded so vulnerable that it ripped at my heart. Couldn't he see how much we needed each other?

"Selling the inn was Grandma's doing, not mine. I'd give it to you if I could, but I can't." My eyes watered and I stepped toward him. "But what's most important is family. You and me. We only have each other now. I . . . I need you."

Suddenly, time froze, and I felt transported back to that awful day at the diner when I'd turned to my brother for comfort. I held my breath, aching for him to put his arms around me like I'd wanted so much when I was little.

He straightened, any emotion wiping from his expression. "You don't need me, Wendy. Or you wouldn't require relationships on *your* terms only. Holidays in Sacramento. Birthday celebrations in Napa or San Francisco. What about our home in Blue Moon Bay? I'll bet Grandma only decided to sell the inn because you never came around. That showed you didn't care about the inn at all."

My stomach roiled and I felt like I was going to hurl. "I-I'm here now."

"Yeah, to sell my home out from under me and then be gone in thirty days." His green eyes flashed with emotion, then glazed slightly. "Thanks a lot, sis. Thanks for *nothing*."

My vision blurred. "Brian—"

"I'm not trying to be a jerk, but I'm wiped and I need this day to end." He ran his hands over his face then moved toward the front doors. "We can talk more some other time. Right now, I need to be by myself. I'll get your bags from the car and put them in your old room."

"Okay . . ." My voice trailed off but I was staring at his backside anyway as he hurried out the double front doors. I closed my eyes and could almost see my grandma in front of me. She would have made things right between Brian and me. But I opened my eyes and saw only the swinging of the door as Brian exited the building. The back of my throat went raw, my eyes burned. Suddenly I gasped, fighting to hold in the ache in my chest that kept expanding despite my efforts. "Air. I need fresh air."

I raced through the lounge and kicked off my heels outside the French doors. Then I ran across the veranda and over the soft grass that stretched out to the bluff. It was dark now. The last of the sun had set but I kept running, trying to get away from all of Brian's angry words. Had he meant what he said? That I only wanted family on *my* terms? Didn't he understand why I stayed away? No, of course he didn't. I'd never told him everything that had happened to me here in Blue Moon

Bay.

The pebbled steps were lighted on either side but I flew down them so fast I tripped over my own feet and pitched forward. I rocketed face-first toward the ground and grasped the railing just in time to keep me from falling against one of the Adirondack chairs at the base of the stairway. Close call.

Balanced once more, I took off again, flying toward the edge of the water, the ocean calling for me to throw myself in. I already felt like I was drowning. Why not make it official? But when my bare foot hit the water, the bone-chilling temperature pierced every pore. Yowzers! Freaking cold Pacific Ocean. Brrr.

I jumped back too quickly though, and fell right on my behind. I watched the water pull back away from my now-turning-numb feet, then the wave rolled in, rushing over my legs and soaking me to the waist.

All of the air left my chest as the icy water braced my legs. That's when I lost it.

My chest convulsed in a last attempt to hold everything in then the first sob escaped, followed by another and another. Tears poured down my face and I dropped my chin to my chest. Now that I'd started, I couldn't stop. I wanted my grandma. The pain of losing her flooded me, and I wailed in a loud way that resembled the sea lions that lived in this coastal town.

Finally, somehow, my outbursts faded to whimpers. My throat had gone raw.

I felt drained, empty, like there was nothing else in me of substance. I might've curled into a ball if I hadn't started shivering so badly. On shaky legs, I stood up and started to brush the wet sand off my rear. It was stuck there, embedded into my slacks.

Slowly, the intense anguish I felt over losing my grandma loosened its hold on me as I brushed sand off my butt. Great, I looked like a freaking mess. At least I was no longer bawling my eyes out, though. But I needed to get cleaned up before Brian saw me. Before *anybody* saw me, really. I hadn't come this unglued since the day I left Blue Moon Bay. Ugh.

Feeling like I'd been run over by a cruise ship, I headed for the steps at the bottom of the bluffs, glancing over at the Adirondack chairs. My heart stopped. A man sat in one of the wooden chairs. Any chance that he hadn't seen me was shot when he stood up.

The yellow glare of the sodium vapor bulbs positioned near the end of the inn's property outlined the man's entire body, which looked like a living, breathing Greek statue. He was tall, six-foot two if I had to guess. He had a broad chest, muscular arms, and his dark hair gleamed under the light of the moon. He didn't look dangerous—probably a guest, staying at the inn since he'd been sitting on one of our chairs.

He was hot—*smoking* hot—and he started walking toward me. I considered tossing myself into the ocean just to hide myself. But it was too late. The damage had been done. I lifted my chin, trying to pull together the tattered remnants of my dignity. For nine years I've been poised and put together and the one time I acted like a raging lunatic, the hottest man on earth decided to show up. Yeah, that cinched my day.

Chapter Two

Standing in front of me was the hottest man I'd ever seen and I must've looked like a complete wreck, given the sand on my booty, the wet pants that clung to my legs, and the streams of black mascara that surely lined my cheeks. So *not* attractive.

He, on the other hand, looked like a cover model who had just stepped out of a fashion magazine. His sky-blue eyes, framed with dark lashes, were ethereal. His chocolate-brown hair blew back from his face, showing off high cheekbones and full lips. He'd rolled his shirtsleeves up, and his shirt was unbuttoned enough for me to get a peek at his broad chest and the suggestion of a very flat abdomen, and he carried a jacket over one shoulder in a raffish way that had my belly doing somersaults—a wildly inappropriate reaction considering I'd just been bawling my eyes out.

Leave it to me to be acting as if I'd lost my mind when the hottest guy on earth decided to show up. I needed to play it cool on the offhand chance he hadn't witnessed my meltdown.

He took a step closer. "I couldn't help but notice you're upset. Is there anything I can do?"

So much for hoping he'd been looking away and plugging his ears. Sigh.

"I'm fine, really." I shrugged, and gestured toward the ocean. "My hysterical twin was just having a hissy fit, but I told her to take a swim."

He didn't laugh like I'd hoped. Instead, his concerned gaze remained on mine. "Are you certain—"

Woof-woof! Woof-woof!

Loud barking came out of nowhere. My gaze shot past the gorgeous man's shoulder in time to see a huge golden retriever barreling toward me at full speed. Adrenaline coursed through me, and my eyes bulged seconds before the dog's massive paws collided with my chest, knocking me down on the wet sand. As I lay back, stunned, a wet tongue swiped across my cheek over and over.

As if being assaulted on the sand by a huge dog wasn't bad enough, the tide rushed back in, and a wave broke right over me. I gasped and choked, flailing like crazy as the heavy furry body weighed me down and bone-freezing water snaked over my body. Suddenly the dog moved away and strong arms lifted me out of the water. I was saved!

I would've loved being cradled in warm, muscular arms if I wasn't coughing and sputtering profusely. My muscular rescuer carried me safely to shore and away from the crazy dog, then he set me down on the Adirondack.

"I'm so sorry." Mr. Heavenly Eyes swooped his jacket around me and rubbed my arms as he spoke. His hands were as strong as I'd imagined they might be. Shivers danced up my spine and they weren't from the chilly water temperature. "Are you okay?" he asked.

I probably looked like a drowned rat, but I managed a weak smile. "Yes, I'm fine," I said, my teeth chattering as I spoke.

He squatted beside my chair and raked a hand through his hair. "That was Lucky. She doesn't usually like strangers. I had no idea she would jump on you. I hope you'll forgive her . . . and me."

Realizing how comical this must've looked, a small

giggle escaped as I wiped my hair from my cheeks, and he tightened his jacket around me. "I'll forgive you both if you'll ignore the fact that I look like a wet rat."

His gaze flicked over my face as if taking all of me in, then he smiled revealing straight white teeth. "You look beautiful, like you've been kissed by the bay."

Oh, wow. Gorgeous, a hero, *and* a sweet talker? This guy might actually be the bright spot in my otherwise awful day. He'd even used the phrase "Kissed by the Bay," reminding me of the local legend I'd believed as a child. . . .

I smiled secretly at the thought, and lifted my gaze to his. "Dogs jump. It's sort of in their DNA. My grandma used to have an Irish wolfhound. She required all of the guests at the inn to sign a paper saying they knew the dog was on the property before they arrived. She was adamant that no 'dog haters' were allowed."

Why had I told that silly story to him? It was true, but I didn't usually discuss Grandma or anything else personal with anyone. Maybe I had hit my head on a particularly hard patch of sand or rock.

He nodded, as if he approved of my grandma's crazy

requirement. "An Irish wolfhound? Those are great dogs, if you can get them to like you. They are fiercely loyal, unlike most people. I guess that's why I love Lucky so much. She's loyal to a fault."

I blurted, "I totally agree that people aren't loyal. Even when they claim they are, they're not." My face heated. Why had I said that to him?

He bent his head as if in thought. Then he asked, "Are you here on vacation?"

I shook my head. "No, are you?"

Woof-woof! Woof-woof!

His gaze shifted to where Lucky made a mad dash down the beach. He laughed as she frisked around in the water. "Maybe I should follow her, so she doesn't *greet* anyone else who might be out here this time of night. Would you like to take a walk?"

A ripple of excitement fluttered through me at the invitation, which surprised me. It wasn't like me to walk alone on the beach with a stranger. But I couldn't resist spending more time with him. After all, he had rescued me from certain tongue licking.

"Yes, that sounds great." I wrapped his jacket tighter

as the wind whipped through me. My feet were bare and the sand was pliant yet firm beneath my feet. Little bits of seaweed clung to my ankles as we walked along the shore, following his gamboling dog. I was a mess, but enjoying every minute of it. "Did you say you were on vacation?"

"No, I'm only here one night. For business." He gave me a side-glance as he walked beside me, and extended his hand. "I'm Max, by the way."

"My rescuer." I took his hand in mine, tingles skittering up my arm. Wowzers. Major sparkage. "I'm Wendy."

"Very nice to meet you, Wendy." He smiled, the corners of his eyes crinkling in a way that made him look even more dashing. Yes, Max could *totally* be a cover model. "If you aren't on vacation then you must live here?" he asked.

Normally I'd give some vague answer to a personal question, but when I gazed up into his eyes, somehow the truth longed to come out.

My facial muscles tightened. "I grew up here, but I don't live here anymore."

He gestured toward the full moon, hanging over the ocean, large and radiant between the thick clouds. "This is a charming town with beautiful views. I'll bet it was an incredible place to grow up."

A small puff of air escaped my mouth as I shook my head, and a lock of damp hair fell against my cheek. "I suppose for some people that's true."

"But not you?" He brushed the moist piece of hair aside, leaving a trail of goosebumps where his skin touched mine.

I closed my eyes, savoring each tingle. "Let's just say the town's charm wasn't enough."

"I see."

The fact that he hadn't pushed made me want to tell him more. Or maybe it was the caring depth to those blue eyes. Either way, instead of changing the subject like I usually would, I hesitated. I'd built a tall wall around my heart to protect myself. But Max didn't know me, and we would likely never see each other again. So what would be the harm in opening up to him? I was tipsy and a little vulnerable, and before I could stop myself, it all came tumbling out.

"We moved here when I was a kid. But my parents? They're a little unusual." I made a motion with my hand and the jacket slipped off my shoulder, but I barely noticed. It felt so good to confide in someone who seemed interested in what I had to say. Unlike Brian. "It's like they couldn't settle down. They still haven't. The last I heard they were either in Malaysia or trying to grow coffee in Hawaii, but I can't keep track."

He repositioned his jacket around me, his arm lingering around my shoulder.

"They just ditched me here when I was a kid." I lifted my lashes to find him peering down at me, his eyes locked on mine. "Both my brother, Brian, and me. He's older. Our grandma owned this inn and they left us with her. So I lived at the inn until I graduated high school. Then I moved away. My brother doesn't understand why I wanted to leave this place. He's pretty mad at me, actually."

His brows rose. "Mad at *you*?"

"I left after graduation and I didn't come back because . . . well, here I'm just Wendy—the girl abandoned by her own parents, and whose boyfriend went off to college then cheated on her and dumped her. In Sacramento, I'm a high selling real estate agent. My Realtor photo is on billboards all over town. I'm *someone* there. Here, I'm just . . . pathetic. I can't believe I'm telling you all of this. I never tell anyone this stuff. I had a few too many beers or maybe I snorted a hallucinogenic starfish when I went under. I'm sorry to unload on you."

He clasped his fist to his chest. "Hallucinogenic starfish? Do they have those here? I'd better get Lucky out of the water."

I had to laugh. "Okay, that starfish thing was pretty far-fetched. But enough about me. Let's talk about you instead. You said you're here for business?"

"Oh right. I was supposed to . . . well, I heard about this possible project. I'm in town to look into it. Next I'm off to Japan. I've always been very career-focused. In fact, I can't remember the last time I took a vacation. Maybe that's why I'm so enchanted with Blue Moon Bay."

His hip bumped against mine, a casual little touch that sent my heart racing. I smiled. "A fellow workaholic. What exactly do you do?"

"I run my own company, with my dad. I do most of my work from behind a computer, which suits me. I travel a lot, too, which has its perks. I'm afraid I'm a bit of a loner." His eyes met mine and we stopped walking for a moment. The water curled over my bare feet and ankles. "You have really lovely eyes, Wendy."

"You do, too." I felt breathless from the way he was looking at me. Was he going to kiss me? If so, I was *not* going to protest.

As we were gazing into each other's eyes, Lucky bounded up, and kicked a few spurts of sand our way. Then she ran back in the direction we'd just walked. I glanced down at my sand-covered slacks and Max grinned. "Are your pants linen?"

"Yes."

"You'll have to send me the dry cleaning bill. Also, it seems you have lost an earring." He tucked my hair back behind my ears. A delicious set of shivers ran through me. His breath was warm against my cheek and he leaned closer. "Yes, it's definitely gone."

Those earrings cost over a thousand dollars. I'd bought them with a commission from a really good sale. I should be upset that one was missing but I was too distracted because Max's chest was almost against mine and his hand was still lying ever so lightly on my shoulder.

Maybe *now* he was going to kiss me . . .?

"Oh, too bad about my earring," I whispered, trying to catch my breath. "Peridot gems are my birthstone, too. It's probably washed out to sea by now."

I leaned a little closer. . . If he didn't kiss me soon, I might have to kiss him.

"I'm sorry." He skimmed his knuckles against the sensitive skin beneath my ear. "You must've lost the earring when Lucky greeted you."

"Who knows? I might've lost it earlier when, you know, my hysterical twin appeared." I let out a small laugh. Being with Max tonight made everything brighter, which sounded so corny to my own mind. But it was also true.

His hand brushed mine one more time, sending a rush of heat in its wake, and then he pulled his hand away. "I'd better catch up with Lucky, so she doesn't get into trouble."

My heart sank with disappointment, which was just crazy. I didn't know this guy, and I'd certainly never kissed a stranger on the beach. What was *wrong* with me? And why hadn't I just planted my mouth on his while I had the chance?

I swallowed, trying to tamp down on my attraction before it got out of control. We started walking again. "So, what were you doing on the Adirondack earlier, all by yourself?"

The corner of his mouth lifted. "I was thinking about the legend of being kissed by the bay. I read about it on a plaque on the other side of the stairs."

I loved that story as a child. I'd read the plaque thousands of times, and had it memorized. I also loved that he'd been thinking about the story—that showed he had a romantic side, which I hadn't witnessed from a guy in a long time.

"The legend is an old story." I glanced out at the moonlight shimmering on the bay. "All of the locals are familiar with it."

"Is the story true?" he asked, his voice husky.

His question made me think. I looked up at the full

moon, remembering when I was twelve, and noticed the summer boy who'd been a guest at the inn, along with his parents. He was cute and adventurous and wild. He'd even climbed over his balcony on the second story and jumped into the pool. Oh, how I'd crushed on that boy.

I used to fall asleep dreaming of kissing him under a blue moon, so we'd be in love forever. But, of course, I'd never kissed him. He probably hadn't even known I existed. Those fantasies were also before I found out what actually happened when you gave your heart to someone.

"Wendy?"

"Sorry." I shook away my thoughts, then shrugged. "I don't know who started the legend, or if the story was true. One thing I do know is that my family has owned the inn for generations, and the rule was never to mingle with the summer folks."

"Do you know I envy you a little? My family doesn't have any stories like that."

I tilted my head. "Tragic stories lead to pain. I'd rather be less familiar with them."

His face sobered and he nodded. "Did you say your

grandma owns the inn?"

"She did." My chest tightened. "She died recently, and she left the inn to my brother and me. She actually put me in charge. My brother's not too happy we're selling it."

Max turned around to look at the inn. "It's an amazing building."

"Yes, but my life is in Sacramento." My tone was sharp and majorly defensive. As soon as the words were out, I wanted to take them back. I sighed. "My brother and I had an argument earlier over selling the inn, and it upset me. That's why my hysterical twin appeared. Because of Brian and my grandma, and from being back in this town again. Being here conjures up all those not-so-good memories."

Great. Now Max probably thought I was beyond weird. I couldn't believe I'd told him so much. For all I knew he might be a serial killer or something, and here I was, pouring my heart out to him like I'd known him forever.

"I feel really stupid right now." I clamped my lips shut and bit my tongue. Hard.

"Why?" He touched my arm as we passed by the stairs I'd run down an hour ago.

I raised a shoulder. "For unloading my life's history on a total stranger."

"Take it easy on yourself, Wendy. You lost your grandmother and you came home for the first time in a long time. I'm willing to bet you're confused and tired and maybe even a little overwhelmed. It happens. Give yourself a break."

Could serial killers be gorgeous and nice? I didn't think so. Most of the ones I'd ever heard of weren't. "You're very sweet to listen."

We walked along in silence. Lucky howled at the full moon, making us both laugh.

"She's a beautiful dog," I said, admiring her reddish-gold coat.

"A sweet one, too." He gazed over at her in an affectionate way. "She'd been tossed out behind a restaurant, just left like garbage. She was skinny, almost starving, and I just couldn't leave her."

Poor Lucky. Although I'd never been without food, I knew exactly what it felt like to be left behind. Not good at all.

To complicate things, I started thinking of Max as a wandering hero, the kind of guy who rescued orphaned dogs and . . . I put a tight lid on that. He might still be a psycho after all. Plenty of nut cases had dogs. Right? Plus, he liked to travel, which reminded me of my parents.

"What are those? Vacation rentals?" Max pointed toward the light glowing from the windows of the mansions on the bluffs.

"Vacation homes, mostly. Some owners rent them out online. There are other owners that live there full time, local celebrities, I've heard."

His hip bumped mine again. I shivered and butterflies took flight in my belly. I could understand my body's reaction, though. Max was the kind of guy who could make a practical woman like me think about romantic sails along sandy shores, long swims on cool waters, and kisses on the beach under the moon.

The cold sand sifted between my toes and it seemed fitting when I spotted the small monument against the bluff, which was the location of the legend that had entertained beach goers of Blue Moon Bay for decades with its story of everlasting love. The rational part of my brain knew it had to be a folktale written by one of my ancestors, but everyone loved this story and it had enchanted me as a child—especially when I'd thought of the balcony-jumping summer boy.

Max and I walked along the beach and stopped when we reached the monument's weathered pillars. Lucky lay down on the sand beneath it and made an ominous whimpering sound that sent chills up my arms.

"Kissed by the Bay." Max's voice was deep, rumbly, and romantic as he read that top line of the plaque with its bronze lettering. The rest of the words had begun to fade into the metal. They were still legible, though, even though I knew them by heart. He continued on in his soothing voice, "One kiss, right here, under a blue moon will lead to love that lasts forever. . . .

"Know the history of two young people, the daughter of locals and the son of summer guests, who fell helplessly in love at this very beach. When their parents discovered their relationship, they were forbidden to see each other. His parents felt the working girl was beneath their son and her parents feared the scandal could ruin their business. But the night before the family was to return home, the son got a note to his sweetheart and they met here under the stars.

"He pleaded with her to wait a year for him to turn eighteen and become a man—that until then they could write to each other in secret and he'd find a way for them to be together. The young girl knew their parents would never allow that to happen, though. She'd always obeyed her parents and wasn't strong enough to go against their wishes, even for the perfect love she shared with him.

"So, with broken hearts, they said goodbye to each other right here at this very spot. A blue moon hung in the night sky, illuminating their final kiss and they promised to love each other always. Then they vowed that everyone who kissed at this exact point by the bay, under a blue moon, would be in love forever—and would never separate as they tragically had."

My gaze stuck to the plaque as a cold breeze swept over my shoulders. What would it feel like to love someone like those people had loved each other? I turned to Max, who faced me at the same time. It was dark, and his handsome features were wrapped in shadows from the moonlight. The water washed against the shore behind us in soothing, rhythmic sounds.

His blue eyes peered down at me. "Do you believe in legends?"

I lifted my lashes. "I used to."

His gaze went upward. "It's a full moon tonight. Do you know if it's a blue moon?"

"It's the second full moon this month, which means it *is* a blue moon." My throat went dry. I wanted him to kiss me, but this was crazy. I barely knew him. "But I don't believe in the legend anymore."

He caressed my cheek. "Are you willing to risk it, though? One kiss, right here, under a blue moon?"

Every ounce of me knew I should run back inside the inn for safety—not from violent danger, but from the perils of opening my heart. Instead of running, though, I found myself whispering, "Yes . . ."

I lifted up on my toes as he moved toward me, then his mouth captured mine. For a moment, panic rolled through me, but I smacked it down. My heart was *not* at risk, because there was no way we would fall in love.

Max was leaving Blue Moon Bay in the morning, so my feelings were completely safe. With that settled, I let myself get lost in the kiss.

His lips were warm, soft, and firm. I leaned into him, breathing in the light and faded cologne—obviously expensive—that wafted up from his neck. His shirt was dry while mine was still damp, and our bodies pressed together as he slanted his head and deepened the kiss.

A small breathy sound escaped me as his tongue stroked along my bottom lip. I should *not* be doing this. Despite my mental reservations, I opened my mouth and tasted him. Oh, yum. Double yum. All of the pain and heartache from today fell away as I focused on Max's delicious kisses that were making my legs turn all soft and noodle-like.

His fingers skimmed lightly down my neck, making me shiver. Our tongues met and parted, then met again. I couldn't believe I was kissing a total stranger right here on the beach but a little voice in my head told me to stop worrying about it. I happily obeyed. The rush of heat flowing through me felt way too good to care about anything else.

The fact that I might never see Max again made my passion grow, and our kisses became hungry as his tongue explored mine. We stood for the longest time, kissing, and finally embracing in a body hug that threatened to unhinge me. I wanted this man, with every fiber of my being, and I didn't know hardly anything about him.

I suddenly wanted the legend to be true, that kissing him at this spot, under a blue moon would make him mine—if only for tonight.

Chapter Three

I woke up to the sound of ocean waves outside my window, and my thoughts on Max. His off the charts hotness still unnerved me and I couldn't get his warm smile or the image of his baby blue eyes off my mind. He had been a lovely escape with his sweet kisses, caring demeanor, and even his crazy dog. But I had other things to focus on now.

I had a thriving real estate business to keep going and an inn I needed to refurbish and sell— over my brother's claims that losing our ancestral estate was entirely my fault. Since Max was leaving today, and I wasn't interested in pursuing a long-distance relationship, I had to get the night before off my mind and face reality.

First, I needed some paint samples so my brother and I could choose the colors to repaint the interior of the inn. Sage or blue might give the place some flair. To face the paint store task, I needed some morning fuel, which meant a coffee and a Danish.

Brian wasn't at the front desk, but I hoped a good

night of sleep had made him see that I wasn't the bad guy here. Maybe I'd bring him back a coffee as a peace offering. I strolled through the front doors of the inn and turned around to stare at the front. I wanted, really, to see it through the lens of a licensed Realtor, but instead I saw it with the eyes of the girl I had been. I felt an unexpected pang in my gut at the thought of it belonging to someone else.

I revved up my Mercedes SUV, then cranked up the radio to a hard rock station, and headed down the highway toward Main Street. Once I'd reached downtown, I saw the familiar sign for Bay Side Coffee, and turned down the cobblestone street. The shops, all pastels and gingerbread, stood neatly in a row, and I found nearby parking against the curb a block away.

When I stepped out of the car, I noticed my favorite taco place was gone, replaced by a surf shop. But the bakery was still there with its tempting treats on full display in the windows. The little dress shop had hats on display. My brother and I used to buy a new one for Grandma on each of her birthdays. She'd loved wearing big hats to keep the sun off her face.

Blue Moon Burgers sat next to the dress shop. When I was a teenager, that burger joint had been the spot where my besties and I hung out every day after school and on weekends. Olivia had once thrown up right in the potted hydrangeas by the front door after two grilled cheese sandwiches, a large fries, and too many chocolate milkshakes.

I'd been sitting in that very restaurant, slurping down ketchup-laden fries, when Megan told me she wanted to be a famous artist—a female Picasso. This was also the diner where Charlie had cried, after a high school cheerleader had stolen away the boy she liked.

Nostalgia struck me. Those had been good days and good friends too. It felt like another lifetime ago. With my career keeping me so busy, I didn't have much time for friends. I went out for drinks sometimes with a colleague or client, and lunches with my assistant. But I hadn't made any close friendships since my high school days, and those relationships immediately died when I left town and my former life behind.

Inside Bay Side Coffee, I was surprised to find a long line at the counter. I took that as a sign that the coffee was good. Two efficient-looking women operated the shop, writing names on cups, and yelling incomprehensible things at each other. The smell of freshly ground beans and steamed milk dominated the air, and I savored the scent.

Once I got to the front, I ordered two twenty-ounce lattes with extra shots of espresso, a couple of pastries, then jostled my way to the end of the counter to wait for my drinks. While waiting, I whipped out my cell to see if any clients had called while I'd been rocking out in the car to an old Van Halen song. No missed calls, but there were four texts from my assistant, Janine, despite the fact that it was only seven in the morning.

"Wendy Watts? Is that really you?" a female voice squealed.

At the sound of my name, I blinked and spun around. In front of me stood a petite blonde with bouncy curls. She wore a tight black tank top, baggy jeans, and her bright amber eyes peered up at me with delight.

My mouth dropped open. "Megan Wallace?"

She lunged forward, and hugged me hard. "It *is* you! I can't believe it."

A rush of emotion overtook me. Megan and I had met the first day of freshman year when the homeroom teacher seated us in alphabetical order. I'd been super shy through elementary and middle school—abandonment issues and all—and hadn't made any real friends. So I was nervous starting high school, but Megan's bubbly personality had put me at ease right away and we became best buddies.

"It's been so long." I laughed, squeezing her back. For such a little person, she had me in quite the bear hug. "How *are* you?"

"I'm great. Just wonderful." Megan's face glowed and she still seemed like the bouncy, peppy girl she'd always been. She kept hold of my arm as she turned to glance over her shoulder. "Look who it is, Olivia!"

"I see her," a female voice said, her tone flat.

I felt my ribs caving in from Megan's grip, but managed to twist around far enough to lock eyes with Olivia, who stood up from the tiny booth she had been sitting in. Megan, Olivia, Charlie, and I had been a tight-knit high school posse.

When we were kids, Olivia's red hair had been her

greatest misery. Now it was her best feature. The frizziness was gone, replaced by long sleek waves that hung down her back like a sheet of molten lava. Strands of gold shot through it, and her blue eyes, always hidden behind thick glasses before, were now peering at me from between a thick set of eyelash extensions.

"You look great Olivia." I pulled her into our group hug, but she didn't seem half as excited to see me as Megan did.

"You look great, too," Megan enthused, attaching her hand to mine. "So grown up and fancy. Yeah, that's the word. Brian tells me you're in real estate and have billboard ads all over Sacramento. He's so proud of you."

I blinked. Brian? Proud of me? Apparently she hadn't heard that I was the sole reason he was losing his home. Um, despite the fact that I had nothing to do with it.

"So what are you doing in town?" Megan asked, then her face immediately fell. "Oh, right. I'm sorry about your grandmother."

"I'm sorry, too," Olivia said, ushering our gathering toward the wall so a couple could get past us to put in their order.

·

"Thanks," I said, my throat tightening. I'd complained about my grandma's strict no-nonsense ways, but they both had loved my grandma too—especially when she'd made us late night snacks when we were cramming for tests. All of these memories were too much. I started to feel claustrophobic and dizzy. "I'm in town to sell the inn, but it needs a little facelift before we put it on the market. In fact, I'd better find out what's up with my coffee and get going. I was just stopping buy to grab a caffeine boost before looking at paint samples."

Megan's eyes went round. "You're selling the inn?"

"Of course she is." Olivia's tone was matter-of-fact. "Why would she hang around here? You just heard how well she's doing in Sacramento. I'm sure she'll be out of here by the end of the week."

I raised a brow. Either she was having some serious PMS issues or she was mad at me, and I guess I couldn't blame her. "I'll be here for a month and we're not selling the inn by choice. We *have* to sell. It's a long story . . ."

One that I certainly didn't want to get into at a small town coffee shop. People had big ears in small towns, and I didn't need our ancestral inn making the hot gossip of the week. The conflict had me itching to take off, but there was something I had to ask first.

I bit my lip. "Have either of you talked to Charlie?"

Megan shook her head. "Not since she married Ronnie Clement. You know, Rex Rockwell? He changed his name once his first song took off. Thought it sounded more like a rock star."

"Yeah, I read about that," I said.

"They're divorced," Olivia added, putting her hand up to the side of her mouth for privacy—well, as much privacy as you can get in a buzzing coffee shop. "Smeared all over the tabloids that he'd cheated on her. According to the rag mags, she literally caught him in the deck hammock with some groupie at their mansion here in Blue Moon Bay."

My eyes narrowed. "No way."

"Yep." Megan brought her hands to her cheeks, completing her exasperated expression. "He bought her a huge summer house here, then he got caught in it."

"Got caught in the summer house?" I knew I had just repeated her words but I could not compute that Ronnie would cheat on her like that. Ronnie had been head over heels in love with Charlie. He'd pursued her for over a year before she'd decided to date him. How could he do that to her?

Megan shook her head. "I'm sure she was devastated, but we lost touch with her when she became all rich and famous. I heard she took Rex to the cleaners in the divorce, and good for her. They didn't have a pre-nup since he was a nobody when they got married. The magazines said he gave her an extra huge settlement to keep her from badmouthing him in a memoir. Rumor has it she's currently living in the mansion on the bluffs. I heard she had the porch ripped off and rebuilt though."

"Wow." I bit my lip, wondering how she was doing. Divorce was terrible enough, but to have the dirty details smeared all over the magazines? So awful.

"Olivia!" the barista called out.

"Finally," Olivia groused, and walked away. I hoped the coffee would improve her mood but she stayed by the counter and sipped her coffee without looking at me.

"Is anything wrong with Olivia?" I asked.

"She's still working at The Market, packaging seafood, so that never puts her in a good mood. But she's just started up her own event planning business, Olivia's Occasions. I think it's going to be huge. Once she builds up some clients, I'm sure she'll be able to quit The Market."

The corner of my mouth rose. "You always were our biggest cheerleader."

She shrugged. "I call them like I see them."

"Megan! Wendy!" The barista heaved several cups onto the counter and gave us a wave that said she was too busy to have us standing around chattering on her watch. We automatically exchanged a secret look, agreeing with our eyes that the barista needed less shots in her coffee.

"It was nice to see you, Wendy." Olivia flipped her fiery-red hair over her shoulder, then faced Megan. "We'd better head out. I need to be at work soon."

"I'm giving Olivia a ride since Chutney broke down again." Megan gave me a look that said that happened quite a bit.

"You still have that car?" I chuckled, since Olivia's parents had bought that little blue sedan for her sixteenth birthday. She'd stained the back seat with chutney soon after during a particularly aggressive make-out session with her high school boyfriend who had bought her Indian food for dinner, but they'd gotten distracted. We'd all laughed about it and Charlie had named the car.

With a sigh, I followed them outside. We exchanged cell numbers and promised to meet for lunch. They gave me their condolences again on losing my grandma. We hugged, then they walked toward Megan's car, and drove off together.

As they turned the corner and disappeared out of sight, I felt surprised that not all of my memories from Blue Moon Bay were horrible. I guess I'd kind of built it in my mind that way after I left. Maybe this was one of the reasons my grandma thought I should return again. If so, I had to admit she was right.

My grandma's death had taught me that I needed to hold on to those I love, and not let myself get lost in only work. I'd missed my friends. I hadn't even realized how much until I'd seen them again. Reconnecting with Megan wouldn't be a problem. But rekindling my relationship with Olivia might prove to be more difficult. I needed to let go of my old insecurities and reach out to her. I just had to figure out how.

****

When I turned down the long driveway at the inn with my paint samples, I thought about how much work was needed on the inn and started to panic. Stress was normal for me. But giving my grandmother's beloved ancestral inn a proper sprucing in only one month? That kind of pressure made me feel something far worse than stress, more like utter terror.

The inn contained five buildings in total and each building had ten rooms—five upstairs and five on the main level. The main building sat in the middle with its grand entry and double doors. Beyond the entry was the lobby, kitchen, dining room, lounge area, library, two offices, and the four bedrooms upstairs that we had lived in. That was a *lot* of space and most of it needed a facelift of some sort. We also needed to do something with the abandoned restaurant on the property that had closed when Mr. Duffy, the owner and chef, had died.

Let's not forget that Brian was sure to be looking over my shoulder, scrutinizing everything I did and blaming me for anything that should go wrong. No added pressure there. Ugh.

I pulled into a parking space next to a luxury convertible, killed the engine, then glanced at the clock on my phone. Just before noon. It was a cowardly move, but checkout was at eleven, so I'd stayed at the paint store longer than necessary to make sure I wouldn't run into Max here on his way out. The thought of never seeing him again left a small hole in my chest, but it was better to rip off the Band-Aid than drag out another good-bye.

Not that I wouldn't love another round of the good-bye kisses he'd given me. Oh, yum. But he was off to Japan or wherever and I'd be back in Sacramento in a month, so there was no point in prolonging the end. That's why I'd declined his offer to keep in touch. Even if we wanted to make something more of this, long distance didn't work. I knew that first hand.

I gathered my samples and the estimates, then strode into the inn. Brian was behind the desk, wearing a badly wrinkled shirt. It was obvious he hadn't shaved yet. It was possible he hadn't combed his hair, either. A guest's impression of the inn started at the lawn and continued all the way through. That was one of Grandma's lessons that had stuck with me all my life. Since Brian knew that, too, it seemed like he wasn't doing so well.

An elderly couple strode in from the hall and I waited until the foyer was empty, before I walked up to my brother, my voice purposely calm. "How are you doing?"

His brows quirked. "Fine. Why?"

I stared at him like he'd grown two heads. "Well, Grandma always said never to come downstairs until we were fresh and looked our best. Do you want me to iron that shirt for you? Or at least get you one that doesn't look like you slept in it?"

His eyes narrowed. "Why are you in such a lousy mood?"

"I'm just trying to help you, but if you don't want my help, then forget it," I growled. He was going to drive away guests by looking like a slob, but whatever. I set the bag with the samples and swatches down on the counter, along with the bag from Bay Side Coffee. Unfortunately, I'd downed his latte after my second hour at the paint store. "I brought you a pastry. It's a beautiful day in Blue Moon Bay, after all."

"Grandma would smack you in the head if she heard

you use that sarcastic tone." He peeked in the little brown bag, than nodded appreciatively. "A bear claw? My favorite."

"I know that's your favorite," I said, hurt that he sounded so surprised. I leaned against the counter and dropped my head in my hands. "It's like I can't do anything right."

"What's wrong?" His tone was firm, like it was when he meant business. "I'd say you're mad at me, but you came in this way. I could tell by the look on your face."

Something wrong? Where should I start? I lifted my head, intending to hold in all that was bothering me, then decided to spill just a little. He was already mad at me. What's the worst he could do? Be *more* mad at me?

"I ran into Megan and Olivia at the Bay Side Coffee," I said.

He popped a piece of the flaky bread in his mouth. "Why is that a problem?"

"Because it made me realize how much I miss them. Megan was great, and she gave me this huge hug and talked a mile a minute. But Olivia was real stand-offish, like she wasn't even happy to see me."

He gave me a look like I was clueless. "Olivia was one of your best friends. When you left you hurt people, whether you meant to or not. Going away to college is one thing, but you never came back to visit or tried to keep in touch. Then you were always too busy with work to meet up with them, and that's bogus. You can't blame her for not welcoming you with open arms."

Wait, since when was my brother insightful? I narrowed my eyes. "Did you talk to Megan?"

He smirked. "She called after she ran into you."

So I wasn't being paranoid about Olivia. She really *was* upset with me. Rather than argue Brian's point about losing touch with my friends, I decided to unload the other problem that was putting my stress level into the red zone.

I inhaled deeply. "How are we going to pay to fix up the inn, Brian? We have to give it a good facelift or it's not going to sell well. In addition to all of the things we talked about last night, I noticed the railings out front are in really bad shape."

"I can fix those. They just need a few strategic nails and a fresh coat of paint," he said, his tone relaxed, as if it was no big deal. When had he become Mr. Chilled Out? He'd been all dark and gloomy last night. Now he was optimistic? Instead of easing any worries, his change in attitude only increased the tension in my chest.

My fists tightened at my sides. "How can you stand there acting all nonchalant? The exterior of the inn needs painting, the shutters need rehanging, the dining room needs fresh linens and new centerpieces—"

"Wendy, you're losing it. Calm down."

Did he not understand the magnitude of getting an inn of this size ready for sale in one month? I gripped the front of his shirt. "Do you realize what could happen if we don't make the estate appealing to an innkeeper?" I swallowed, barely able to say the words that I knew from my experience in real estate. "A developer might buy the property for the location, tear down the inn, and build a huge five-star resort or something here."

Brian went pale. "Are you nuts? We can't sell the inn to some developer! This place has always been here and it should be here forever—like a Blue Moon Bay landmark."

He was sounding as hysterical as me now. Was it

totally wrong that I preferred him freaking out the way I was? Misery loves company and all of that?

"I couldn't agree more." I released his wrinkled shirt and splayed my fingers flat on the counter. "But even if we can get everything done in time, funding the renovations will be a major issue. Most of my income I put back into my business. I have some savings, but I need it for the townhome I want to buy that's coming on the market any day now."

"I have some savings." He leaned onto his elbows, so his eye line was straight with mine. "Not much. But I know some guys, so maybe I can get us a deal on the exterior painting."

"What about everything else?"

"I went over the books this morning." He gestured toward the pile of papers next to him. "Grandma had a small insurance policy that covered burial expenses but not much else. There's some money in the bank, but not enough for the rest of the renovations." His chin jutted out. "We can't sell this place to a developer, though."

"What else can we *do*?" I practically shrieked.

A family came down the hall with their luggage and I

stepped back, smiling as brightly as possible. "I hope you enjoyed your stay," I warbled.

The guy shot me a strange look, then he asked Brian about the local winery tours, while the woman with him tried to contain their two young children who were jumping around the lobby like hyenas. Grandma would've calmed the kids down by giving them each a cookie and telling them they had to sit on the bench while they ate them. I didn't even have a stick of gum. I was such a failure as an innkeeper.

The man thanked Brian, lifted his suitcases, and headed out the door with his family. I glanced at the time on my phone, and panic rolled through me. "It's way past eleven. Why are the guests only leaving now instead of an hour ago?"

"Well, sis, that's a little thing we like to call a late checkout. Good customer service keeps the guests happy and coming back year after year," he said, enunciating every word like I didn't understand plain English.

"Late checkout?" I repeated, every muscle in my body growing taut. "You didn't, um, happen to give anyone else a late checkout? Did you?"

He sighed, throwing his gaze at the ceiling. "No, but who cares if I did? It's not like we have a full book or anything. Are you going to be micromanaging me the entire month? If so, warn me now so I can buy some earplugs."

I ignored his smart remark and let out the breath I'd been holding. If everyone else had checked out already, that meant Max was gone. Instead of feeling relief, though, the little hole in my chest grew bigger. It was sure to pass, though. I hoped.

"Are you okay?" Brian asked.

"No," I admitted, tired of holding in my feelings any longer. I'd been doing that for too many years. It was time to let go of my insecurities and just say how I felt. I sucked in a breath for courage. Here went nothing. "You may have issues with me because I moved away, but there is too much at stake for us not to work together right now."

He held his palms up. "Look, Wendy—"

"No, I'm emotionally involved in the sale of real estate, which is exactly what I tell my clients *not* to do." I'd cut him off and continued, but I needed to get this out.

"But how can I not be emotionally involved? This was our family's ancestral inn, and now we're going to sell it to the highest bidder. This is so not right and it's hard to believe this nightmare is really happening. I know you blame me for what Grandma did in her will. I want you to know if I could go back in time and talk with her about it, I would."

The vein on his temple throbbed, but he kept his gaze on me. He was listening.

"I'd tell Grandma how much the inn means to you, to *both* of us." I saw his green eyes shimmer, and he pressed the pads of his fingers to the corners of his eyes. My throat started to close, but I managed to keep going. "But I can't go back in time, Brian. I missed my chance. You're right that I messed up by staying away. I was blocking out the most important people in my life, because I was afraid of getting hurt again."

To anyone looking in from the outside, my life in Sacramento was a huge success. I was proud of my accomplishments, but now I realized I'd shut out the most important thing in life—relationships. I pictured the elegant townhouse I wanted so badly. I'd saved for years and it was supposed to go on the market soon. But how could I live there happily if it meant tearing down my family's beloved inn to buy it? Suddenly, I knew what I had to do.

"I'm sorry for shutting you out, but you shut me out first." My voice cracked as I said the words. "When I was eight, I needed my big brother's comfort and you pushed me away. I avoided this town like the plague because I was trying to protect myself. I *never* meant to hurt anyone." I swiped under my eyes, gathered my composure, and lifted my chin. "I have a large down payment saved for my townhouse, and I'll use it for the inn renovations. After the sale, we can reimburse my account with the proceeds."

The pulsing on Brian's temples increased to a rapid tempo. "What if your townhouse goes up for sale? What will you do then?"

I closed my eyes, dizzy at the thought of losing the townhome. I'd worked my entire adult life to save for a stable home that would be permanent and mine. The townhome was beautiful, close to work, and in the exact area I wanted near my office.

"Let's just hope it doesn't go on the market yet. We'll work as quickly as possible to get the place ready for a buyer who will see the inn's unique charm, and continue to run this quaint and quirky inn for generations to come. We owe that to Grandma."

His face contorted and he blinked rapidly. "I don't know what to say. . . Thank you, Wendy."

"You're welcome," I said, feeling hopeful that our relationship was starting to move in the right direction. I lifted my arms, about to reach for my brother, when a flash of reddish-brown appeared in my peripheral vision and a large golden retriever bounded into the lobby, tongue hanging out of its mouth as it sprinted toward me.

Two paws met my chest at the same time as I put one foot back to steady myself, and I managed not to go down this time as Lucky greeted me with her wet kisses.

"Down, girl!" a familiar male voice echoed through the room—*Max.*

His presence filled the room and every sensitive nerve in my body heightened, causing pressure in my chest that made it difficult to breathe. Lucky obeyed her master's command somewhat by dropping down on all four paws, then she pushed her muzzle against my hip, almost purring like she was a cat instead of a dog.

"Hello, Wendy," Max said, his two words sending images of last night running through my mind. Soft kisses. Sweet murmured words. His breath against my neck. . . .

A rush of tingles traveled up my spine. Somehow, I managed to face him. The corners of his mouth rose, and his lips were so familiar I could almost feel them against my skin. Shiver.

"Hello, Max." I managed to keep my voice calm, masking the skittering emotions running through me. What was he doing here still? There weren't supposed to be anymore late checkouts, so he should've been gone.

"Hey, Max." Brian reached toward the old pegboard behind the desk where room keys hung neatly in a row. Grandma had never believed in those slick little plastic cards with the magnetic strips that were so popular now. "Your room is all clean and ready. Glad you'll be staying on with us for the next month."

My entire body froze. What the . . . ?

Max would be staying here for the month? What

about his business? What about traveling to Japan? So many questions reeled through my brain, but one more prominent than the rest: What had I just gotten myself into?

Chapter Four

There were many reasons that hooking up with a hot stranger on the beach was not a good idea, but I never could've imagined having him stick around would be one of them. If I ever thought I would see Max again, I wouldn't have opened up to him about my life's history. He knew my parents had abandoned me, and that Ian had cheated on me in college—the second trauma I'd never even told my best friends. It was too pathetic.

Our talk on the beach and moonlight kisses had been a much-needed heavenly respite. But having Max stay at the inn for the next thirty days? Not acceptable when he knew all of my baggage. He had to go to another hotel. That's all there was to it.

Wrapping my hand around Max's elbow, I guided him across the lobby, trying to get him out of Brian's earshot. Unfortunately, my brother trailed along behind us, stopping nearby to browse through the guestbook. Not too obvious he was eavesdropping.

I pasted on a strained smile. "I hope you've had a

pleasant stay at the inn, Max. But didn't you say you were checking out this morning?"

"Change of plans." A mischievous glint appeared in his beautiful baby blues. Oh, wow. Max looked even hotter in daylight. He'd put on jeans that hugged him in all the right places, and his tee shirt fit snugly across his broad chest. Casual-sexy was a divine look on him. "I've grown fond of this charming little town and I'd like to get to know it better," he added.

A flutter rippled through my belly. Was that a cute way of saying he wanted to get to know *me* better? While I was flattered—and a little giddy—I also knew there was no point in starting anything with him, since we'd both be going our separate ways in thirty days.

"I'm glad you're enjoying the town, but I think another hotel would be a better match for you. We're going to be doing a lot of renovations here this month, which will be very messy. I'm afraid it will be too complicated if you stay here. Sorry." I fiddled with the peeling paint on the windowsill. It had taken all of my effort to force the words out, but I knew it was for the best.

The corner of his mouth hitched up. "Do I look like the kind of guy who would be scared away by a few messy renovations?"

My gaze flicked to his and an electric zing zapped my belly. Heat flooded through me. Suddenly, it was way too hot in here, and I was having trouble breathing. I turned to the windowsill and yanked it open hard. The window shot up too fast, hit the resistance at the top, and the glass fell out in slow motion and crashed against the back porch. Oops.

"You broke the window." Brian came up beside Max and me, and stared at the shards of glass sprinkled across the ground below. "That's going to costs us."

"You think?" Sarcasm dripped from my tone, but he was so not helping the situation. My blood pressure soared so high it was a miracle my head didn't explode.

Max wore a sinful grin. "Do you have any plans for dinner?" he asked, appearing unaffected by the fact that I'd asked him to relocate and had broken a window because he'd flustered me.

"The dining room is closed," I said, firmly. Then I tore my gaze from his lips, wishing I didn't know how good that sexy mouth felt against mine, and scooted away from the now-drafty window frame.

"We really did have to shut the dining room down," Brian chimed in, as if he were a welcome part of our conversation. "The chef died. Keeled over on his halibut special one day. He was the restaurant owner, too. Great guy."

"Sorry to hear that." Max shifted uncomfortably, and an odd look crossed his face that made me wonder what he was thinking. Not that I would ask. A line formed between his brows and he followed me over to the front desk. "I'm asking you out, Wendy. You know, on a date? Somewhere without hallucinogenic starfish . . . ."

A tiny giggle escaped, then I cleared my throat. "No, thanks."

"Hey, sis." Brian crooked his finger at me. "I couldn't help but overhear. In case you think of changing your mind, don't forget the Cardinal Rule. Grandma always said *not* to get involved with the guests." He turned to Max. "No offense."

"None taken." Max slipped his hands in his pockets, and rocked back on his heels.

I threw my brother a harsh look, and he thankfully left the room. I turned back to Max. "I'm sorry, I thought you were leaving today. How can we make that happen?"

His gaze traveled down my body, all the way to my toes, then back up again, resting on my mouth. "The view was too beautiful, so I decided to stay for the month."

Oh. My. Heat sizzled between us, and it was way too hot in here again. I snatched the empty paper Bay Side Coffee bag, and waved it across my face like a fan. Unfortunately, the opening of the bag wasn't sealed and crumbs spewed everywhere, including my face. Just my rotten luck. Trying to hide my face with the bag, I picked bear claw remnants off my eyelashes. What were the chances Max hadn't seen me pelt myself with pastry crumbs? I glanced up.

He grinned at me. "You're blocking my view."

"Wendy likes to hide." Brian breezed through the room carrying a plastic tarp and duct tape. "Once we get the inn ready to sell, she'll hightail it back to Sacramento where she doesn't have to deal with things like family or old friends or bothersome memories."

My fists balled. "Brian—"

"Hey, wait up." Max raised his brows then followed Brian over to the windows. "What kind of renovations are you planning to make? I used to flip houses and did a lot of the work myself."

The two of them began discussing everything from stripping floors to painting the walls. Brian was acting like Mr. Cheerful, making it obvious he preferred Max's company to mine. Whatever.

"Black tea and a little oil will go a long way to making that wood shine." Max gestured to the lobby's floors, then fist bumped Brian before sauntering over to join me at the front counter again.

The paint colors were a blur in front of me. "Why are you staying, Max?"

"Isn't it obvious?" He grinned, propped his forearms against the desk, and leaned toward me. He slipped his hand around mine. "A beautiful woman I met on the beach changed my mind about leaving. I'm finally taking that vacation I've put off far too long."

My skin hummed against his, and I wanted to curl into him. But I resisted. "Look, you seem like a really nice guy. But it wasn't like me to kiss a stranger on the beach or to talk about the stuff we talked about. I'm in town to sell this inn, which is going to be a lot more work than I anticipated. That is what I need to concentrate on, not a fling with a man who will be gone from my life in thirty days. I hope you understand."

He opened his mouth to respond, just as my cell phone buzzed. "Wendy—"

"Excuse me." My cell screen displayed "Megan Wallace" and I'd never been so grateful for an interruption in my life. "Hi, Megan," I said, mustering up as much enthusiasm in my voice as I could, which was difficult with the sinking feeling in the pit of my stomach. Turning down Max had *not* been easy. "What's going on?"

"Not too much." Her peppy voice came through the receiver. "Just calling to see if you wanted to hang out with me tonight. We could scarf down Mexican food, shoot some pool, and catch up?"

I turned to face the wall for privacy. "I'd love to meet you for dinner. I have some things to do around the inn, and then I have to catch up on work after that. How's eight o'clock?"

"Eight sounds good. I'll see if Olivia can come, too. Meet you at Frankie's Fiesta?"

I chuckled. "That place is still around? Okay, see you there." I hung up, and turned around to find Max directly in front of me. He'd come around to my side of the counter this time and stood mere inches away.

He cupped my chin, then came closer. "You just wrecked our dinner plans."

The air left my chest. "We, uh, didn't have dinner plans."

"We were still in negotiations." He grazed my jawline with his fingers, then slipped his thumb behind my earlobe, sending good bumps down my neck. "You're not wearing earrings today."

"I didn't bring any others, besides the one I lost . . ." I spoke as if in a trance, as if under his spell. I could feel his breath against my cheek, and it took every ounce of willpower not to lean into his arms. I licked my bottom lip, inhaling deeply. "Look, you're sweet and an insanely good kisser. But I'm hanging on by an emotional thread right now. I just need to fix up my inn. That's all I have the energy for right now. So, let's just forget last night ever happened. Okay?"

Something flickered in his blue eyes. Then he bent his head, and leaned toward me, his breath tickling my cheek. "You're an impossible woman to forget, Wendy."

Chills vibrated through me and I stopped breathing. He was so close I was ready to forget everything I'd just said and press my mouth to his. Just as I was about to do that, he pulled back and smiled at me. I wanted to protest. But he called to Lucky, who zipped to his side, then they disappeared down the breezeway into the attached building.

My legs felt weak and I was still in a mesmerized zone when a car swung into the circular drive and began honking wildly. I didn't know if it was guests arriving or what, but their horn blared like a tsunami warning.

"The Smithfields." Brian patted the edge of the plastic he'd taped to the window frame, then came over and set his unused supplies on the desk. "Every time they arrive for the weekend, they rattle on about how we should have a doorman out front. I'll collect their luggage and *open* the door, because it's apparently more trouble than they can manage." He paused as he walked toward the double doors. "You okay?"

"Fine." I started flipping though paint samples, hoping Brian wouldn't see how Max had affected me. After all, intense attraction to a gorgeous man did *not* mean I needed to act on my feelings. Although, it would feel *so* good. . . .

The phone shrilled on the desk, jolting me out of my spell. I glanced through the glass panels of the double doors and saw Brian greeting an older couple outside their luxury SUV. The phone rang again, so I snatched it off the cradle. "The Inn at Blue Moon Bay. How may I help you?"

"Wendy?" A familiar female voice came through the line.

My face went numb and all of the blood rushed to my head. I hadn't heard that voice in years, but I *knew* it all too well."

"Wendy? Is that really you?" she shrilled.

"Yes, it's me." I gulped, swayed on my feet, and my hand shot out to clutch the edge of the desk for support. If I hadn't been holding onto the counter I seriously would've fallen. On the other end of the line was my mother.

****

Never in my life have I regretted answering the phone, until now. I hadn't talked to my parents in three years, not since Grandma had forced me onto the phone after a holiday dinner. That conversation had been short and curt. Why was my mom calling me now?

Oh wait, she wasn't calling *me*. She was calling the inn—probably to give her condolences about my grandma. But that still didn't change that I was stuck talking to her. A flood of grief rushed in and anger came hard on its heels. I reminded myself I was a grown woman now and she couldn't hurt me anymore.

So why was it painful just hearing her voice?

I heard Lucky barking outside on the back porch. My gaze darted out in time to see Max walking down toward the beach with a Frisbee in hand. As they went down the steps, his large frame got smaller and smaller, then he disappeared from my sight altogether. I wanted to yell at him to come back.

"Wendy, honey, how are you?" Mom asked.

My brows drew together. Was she serious? Was she

freaking calling me *honey?* I grabbed a dust cloth that someone, probably Brian, had abandoned, just like the woman on the phone had abandoned me. I needed to clean something, and I needed to clean it now.

"Wendy? Are you there?"

"Yes, I'm here. What do you need?" My fingers tightened around the phone, and I dusted with fervor like nobody had ever dusted before. With the cloth gripped tightly in my hand, I rubbed aggressively against the chair rail molding behind the desk.

"It's so good to hear your voice. How have you been?"

"How have I *been?*" I smacked the cloth down, which sent a flurry of dust upward into my nose. I sneezed so hard I was sure I had lost part of my brain. In the back of my mind, I could hear my grandma telling me to be polite. "I'm fine, thank you," I said, instead of hanging up.

"Good. That's good." An awkward silence ensued. Then she made a humming sound like she was thinking of something to say. "I know you're probably busy now that you're back in town, so I don't want to keep you. But

I was wondering if you're still dating the man you met on that reality show? The one who's a Realtor, too?"

Oh, great. She'd watched the show? It figured she'd seen the most humiliating thing I'd ever done in public. Well, except for falling on my booty and crying my eyes out in front of Max. But at least I'd had amazing kisses after that last one.

"No, I'm not dating Chase anymore." I furiously dusted a tiny shelf filled with seashells of varying shapes and sizes. I flexed my hand, unsure if cleaning was relieving my anxiety or increasing it.

"Oh, that's too bad. Your grandma and I weren't sure he was a great match, though. He seemed too focused on work."

She'd discussed the show with Grandma? I knew they talked on the phone every month or so, but I hadn't known they discussed *me*. So not right.

I cleared my throat. "This phone call must be costing you a fortune. I should let you go."

"No, we have that service that lets you call everywhere for cheap," she said, emphatically. "Tell me, did you ever sell that one house? The big brick one with the pillars?"

How had she known about that sale? I'd been so excited about that commission and had told Brian and Grandma, of course. One of them had obviously ratted me out. "Yes, it sold."

I walked toward a large picture, a charming print of a girl running on a beach at sunset, her shadow trailing out behind her. I'd fallen in love with the painting when we'd first arrived at the inn, and I remembered running down the beach looking for my shadow behind me.

Soon after, my parents had moved away.

"I'm sorry, but I have to go now." I pressed my fingers to my temple. My dark memories were far too close to the surface, and I preferred them buried deep where I didn't think of them.

"I understand." Her voice was soft, and tinged with sadness. She paused a moment. "Well, do you know why Brian called? We just got back from camping on the beach under a palm tree. Hawaii's lovely, the culture is simple, like life should be. Anyway, we had a message from Brian to call right away. He said it was important."

Oh, no. That meant they didn't know about Grandma.

How could I be the one to tell her? But I couldn't get Brian, since he was helping guests, and I couldn't make her wait until he had time to call her back.

I sucked in a breath. "Yes, I know why Brian called you. We have bad news to tell you. The worst."

"What's wrong?"

I brought the picture to my forehead, the glass covering cool against my skin. "It's Grandma. She . . . passed away."

"Barbara?" Her voice quavered. "Sh-She passed away? She *died*?"

I closed my eyes, seeking calm in the darkness. "Yes, she's gone. That's why I'm here."

"Oh, no. That's not possible. I just spoke to her last week before our trip and she was fine. She had bought a new hat. Brown, I think she said. She was going to use it for gardening . . ."

"She didn't want a service," I said, making a mental note to look for that hat. She'd loved hats, and that was the last one she ever picked out. I'd keep that hat forever.

"What happened?" Mom asked.

"Heart attack. In the middle of her weekly pinochle

game, too."

Mom sniffled. "Do you know if she was winning? She loved to win."

I dusted harder. "Can anyone win at pinochle?"

"Of course they can, Wendy. Oh, I hope she was winning. I can't believe she's passed on. She had a hard way about her, but I owed her so much. She did me a great big favor—"

"Please don't. I can't go through this with you." I set the picture back down, remembering the day we had arrived at the inn. Mom had looked around with her cheeks all rosy and a smile on her face. She'd said: "This is it! I could stay here forever!"

What a big fat lie. I'd believed her though. Stupid me. Tension rose inside me and I twisted, trying to shake it away. My elbow connected with a vase, which shot to the floor with a sharp crash and shattered. Another casualty. Ugh.

"We need to lean on each other during our time of grief, Wendy. I cared about her like you did. She was a marvelous woman and she . . . I was indebted to her."

"You were indebted to her because she took care of

your kids when you didn't want to," I snapped, tension still coiling inside me so tight I thought I might burst.

"Of course we wanted to, Wendy. But you both grew tired of traveling, so we did what we thought was best. I tried to keep in touch with you, and stay close. You're the one who cut off all communication when you went off to college."

"Well, you were the first to go. Weren't you?" I snapped. They had left us two decades ago, and I should be over that by now. Only I wasn't. Not even close.

"I'm sorry you're upset. Your father and I found it prudent to allow you a safe and stable home like you wanted. But, please. It's time to let the resentment go."

"Let go of the fact that you abandoned me?" I banged the phone against a table a few times. It didn't make me feel better. "Look, Mom, call back later and talk to Brian. I'm sure he would love to reminisce with you."

I heard a noise behind me, and whipped around to find Max standing in the doorway, a trapped expression on his face. He pointed to the Frisbee that had flown through the door, and gave me an apologetic look. Had he overheard my conversation? Oh, I hoped not.

Despite my attempt to get her off the phone, my mom kept talking about good times with Grandma. I clutched the phone in nerveless fingers as he walked toward the Frisbee, Lucky in tow. Her tail wagged and she stopped long enough to lean against my knee. I patted her head with the dust cloth, and she sneezed. Yeah, this place needed a good cleaning.

I wanted to hang up on my mom, but in the back of my mind I heard Grandma's gruff voice saying, "Straighten up and act like you have some manners. Talk to your mother, young lady."

"You know I'm not at all surprised you went into real estate," Mom said, then there was silence. "Your grandma always knew the value of land. Maybe you inherited that from her."

"Maybe." It actually touched me that I might be like Grandma in that way. But why wouldn't she leave me the *choice* to keep the inn or sell it? Or give it to Brian? That's what I didn't get.

Max grabbed the Frisbee, then straightened, and gave me another apologetic look. He started to walk out, and as he passed by he gently squeezed my shoulder. Warmth infused my insides, making my burdens feel lighter. I stared after him, astounded. He hadn't said a word and his small gesture had made me feel better. Incredible.

"I wish I could fly out and be with you both. You know money has never been an easy thing to come by, and it seems that lately there's been less than usual."

She was broke, which didn't surprise me. Before Grandma, we'd hardly had any money growing up. There had been way too many rice or ramen and nothing else nights at our dinner table, but she and Dad had always said life experience would fill us in a way food couldn't.

I sighed. "That's too bad. I can't pay for your flights, because I'm using my savings for renovations on the inn. Otherwise we won't get a good selling price."

"You're selling the inn?" she said, sounding horrified. "Why?"

"Yes, Mom. It's a long story."

"Your grandma loved having you both there at the inn." Mom's voice went stiff, like she was trying to keep her emotions together. "You two made her life so much richer and fuller. I'll let your father know the sad news, and see what we can do about getting there."

I wouldn't hold my breath. They'd never been there for me before. "Well, good luck finding the money for the airline tickets. I'm sorry to have had to deliver such sad news. I'll tell Brian you called. Bye."

"Bye, Wendy. Our hearts are with you."

What good was her heart when they were a gazillion miles away? Like always, I felt let down. After I hung up, I stared at the phone, my head ringing with exhaustion and stress. Through the open doorway, I saw Max watching me, and wondered if he'd heard more of our conversation. He raised his brows in question.

I shook my head, wanting to be alone. He wore a look of understanding as he nodded, then he threw the Frisbee and Lucky bounded after it. Max gave me a small smile, then went after her. I felt awful, horrible, and for some strange reason all I wanted was for Max to come back so I could tell him everything.

Chapter Five

I dropped the rag I'd been cleaning with, leaned against the desk for support, and brought the heels of my hands to my eyes. Talking with my mom made me feel eight years old again, as if my parents had just abandoned us. All I wanted to do was put that behind me. But all those feelings were dredged up again whenever I heard my mom's voice, as did being here at the inn.

"You know what all that honking was about?" Brian appeared in the lobby, pushing a luggage cart piled high with matching designer suitcases. "The Smithfields wanted to drop off their bags. Now they're meeting friends at the golf club. Rough life."

I stepped in front of his cart, raising both my palms. "Whoa, bro. You just missed a call from Mom. I haven't talked to her in years, but somehow I had to be the one to tell her about Grandma? What's not ringing fair about this?" I asked, circling my index finger in the air around my temple.

His forehead wrinkled. "How was I supposed to

know you'd answer the phone?"

"You could've warned me she was going to call!" I snapped.

He flinched, then ran a hand over his face. "Maybe I should've warned you. But you haven't talked to her in years. What's the big deal?"

"How can you ask me that?" I snatched a pad of paper and a pen from inside the front desk. "It's hard enough being here and dealing with Grandma's death. On top of that, I don't need to add Mom telling me that she and Dad dumped us in our own best interest."

"You can't avoid them forever. One day you'll have to deal."

"I'd rather concentrate on things that *can* be fixed." I gestured toward the back door with the pen. "If you need me, I'll be checking the inn's exterior condition. FYI, you're on phone duty the rest of the month." I turned and walked out the door onto the back porch.

As I stepped outside, Lucky bounded up, her reddish-brown ears flopping wildly. She had the Frisbee wedged into her mouth, and tilted her head in a way I couldn't resist. "Drop it, sweet girl," I said, and she opened her mouth to release the slobber-coated disk into my fingers. I smiled, got a good grip on the edge with my thumb, and threw it as hard as I could. The Frisbee soared up momentarily, arched sharply, then dove toward the ground at high speed.

Uh, yeah. Frisbee throwing? Not my forte.

Lucky didn't seem to care about my ineptitude, though. She just dashed after the Frisbee with her tongue hanging out of her open mouth. Where was Max? I glanced around then spotted him bent over the railing, gazing out at the magnificent ocean view. My gaze drifted south and I noted the view of his backside was pretty spectacular as well. I looked for longer than I should have, but was it my fault his snug shorts fit him to perfection? Um, no.

Max straightened, brought his thumb and index finger between his lips, then whistled. Lucky ran over to him, pushing the Frisbee at him. He tossed it effortlessly in the air, and it sailed gracefully across the porch at hip level. Whatever. He'd had more practice. As Max turned, our eyes connected, and he caught me staring at him. Oh, embarrassment. His eyes searched mine. "Hey, beautiful.

What are you up to?"

"I'm inspecting the exterior of the building." I gestured toward the pad in my hand, and smiled. Just being near Max made me feel better, which couldn't lead to anything good. Sigh. Time to go.

"You looked upset on the phone." Max caught up with me as I reached the side of the building. "Was the conversation that bad? I mean, you don't have to talk about it but if you do want to . . ."

"On a scale of one to ten, with ten being the worst, I'd rate it a forty." I gave him a side-glance, before I stopped at the railing, and stared out at the incoming waves. The wind whipped against my hair, blowing the dark strands against my face. "I haven't talked to my mom in years, and now she claims that leaving us here with Grandma was *my* fault. Can you believe that?"

"That's rough." He blew out a breath, shaking his head. Then he twisted toward me, tucking a lock of hair behind my ear. "Is there anything I can do for you?"

His fingers lingered, skimming along my jawline. I sighed, loving his tender gesture. "Not unless you have connections to the Hawaiian gods, and can make coconuts rain on my parents' tiki hut."

He chuckled softly, the sound soothing my frazzled nerves.

I squinted one eye, and peeked up at him with the other. "I'll bet your parents are nice and normal and you don't understand any of my problems."

His fingers pressed together, forming a teepee. "Define normal."

"The opposite of mine." I laughed. Lucky joined in, barking wildly. Then she spun in a circle, and howled before running up the path alongside the railing.

"Well, my parents aren't wanderers like yours. But they have their issues. My parents built their company, The Huntington Group, from the ground up in San Francisco. They invest in real estate, sometimes they buy the land and build, other times they renovate. But instead of stopping to enjoy their success, my parents are ruthless about the next project. My dad is pressuring me to do a specific project with him, but I'm not sure it's right for me. He's not pleased with my resistance."

Huntington? Why did that name sound familiar? I racked my brain, then it hit me, and I snapped my fingers.

"You know what's interesting? I just saw a home reality show called 'Building the Huntington Mansion' about real estate magnate Maxwell Huntington III . . ."

Wait. . . Maxwell? *Max!* No, that wasn't possible. My gaze flicked to his, and I saw the answer in his sky blue eyes. "You're not . . .?"

"Maxwell Huntington IV? Yes, I am."

I stared at him, dumbfounded. "Your parents own The Huntington Mansion in San Francisco?"

He slipped his hands into his pockets. "That's where I grew up."

Oh, I was mortified. Here I was moaning about fixing up this inn to sell, when his parents flipped buildings ten times this size without breaking a sweat. "That mansion is a San Francisco landmark. That's your family? You host *the* party of the year on the 4th of July, with its amazing view of the Golden Gate Bridge and the fireworks."

"Don't be fooled by a beautiful façade." His eyes dimmed slightly, and he glanced down the path where Lucky was sniffing the potted planters. "I love my parents, but they raised me to be who *they* wanted me to be. They're extremely successful, but also competitive people, who take those two things so seriously they don't really think about anything else. It's hard."

"Huh." I tilted my head, wondering what was wrong with being driven at work. That was my specialty.

"Truthfully, I've never thought about much besides work either. I was ready to sign the contract with my dad on a new project, but ever since I arrived at the inn, something has stopped me. I get a feeling here . . ."

"What do you mean?" I asked, amazed at the passion in his eyes.

"It's hard to describe." He gazed at me a moment, then slipped an arm around me and we started walking down the path again. "All I know right now is that when I woke up this morning to the smell of the ocean and the sound of the waves, I felt happier than I've been in a very long time."

"This place is special," I said, thinking the person next to me was pretty special too. I should probably duck out of his arm, but it felt so right being this close to him. I couldn't believe he'd opened up to me like that, and from the seriousness in his tone, I got the feeling he didn't do it often. "You grew up with both parents, which was all I'd ever wanted. But it turns out life wasn't perfect for you either. It's making me wonder if my childhood would've been better or worse if my parents had stayed."

We walked in silence as we rounded the corner, and the inn's Olympic-size pool came into view. Two adults occupied the lounge chairs, and several kids swam in the heated water. Max's hand caressed my side, and a jolt of electricity whipped through me.

Trying to downplay the feelings growing inside me, I gazed up to the balcony, and was reminded of my crush on the cute boy who had jumped off into the pool. I'd been too shy to talk to him, but he'd been a summer boy, just passing through.

I hadn't been too shy with Max, but he was only passing through as well. For a moment, I considered that we might have an amazing month, filled with walks on the beaches, and sails on the bay. But what would be the point? He and I came from different worlds. Plus, my home was in Sacramento, and he traveled all over the world for his business. Nothing could ever come of this, so better not to start something that could only end painfully.

Lucky ran to the edge of the pool, sniffing the water.
Max laughed, and I took that moment to step away from
him. His face sobered and his gaze shot to mine with a
questioning look.

"I like you, Max." I took another step back, but
looked him in the eye, so he'd know how serious I was,
and how much I regretted what I was about to say. "I'm
not going to lie and pretend I don't have feelings for you.
But that doesn't change anything. I have enough
complications in my life right now, so we can't see each
other any more. I've made up my mind."

"I've made up my mind, too." He tucked another
piece of my hair behind my ear, then grinned. "Have a
good dinner with your friend tonight, beautiful. I'll see
you tomorrow."

My mouth dropped open as I watched him walk
away. He called for Lucky, who ran to him, with her
Frisbee. He smiled back at me, then continued down the
path with her. I gaped after him. Had he not heard what
I'd said about us *not* seeing each other again? Let alone,
tomorrow?

Max was a good guy and I knew it. But did he have the right idea about tossing away a lucrative business contract, because the sound of the ocean made him happy? Was happiness more important than success?

After thinking about it, I decided it wasn't. My parents believed their happiness came first, and look what they'd done to their kids. I needed to focus on work, just like my grandma had taught me, so I could buy the stable home I'd always wanted. If Max came around me again, I'd just have to stay strong, and keep my emotional distance—despite what my heart urged me to do.

Chapter Six

I arrived downtown at eight o'clock that evening to meet Megan and Olivia, resolved to make our get together as short as possible, so I would be fresh to focus on the inn renovations tomorrow. It made me sad to limit my time with them, but I needed to stay focused on what I came to Blue Moon Bay to do: sell the inn and go back home to buy the townhome I wanted.

I parked the car and got out, noting the nightlife in the downtown area had been revitalized since I'd left. Numerous sidewalk cafes were open that had been closed earlier in the day. Now, with cute little wrought-iron tables and chairs sitting out front and music playing, the street took on a quaint but electric attitude.

The music was light and upbeat, straight instrumental versions of current pop hits. Tourists and locals alike crowded the sidewalks, some window-shopping in front of the antique stores and surf shops, others perusing the menus displayed outside the entrances to restaurants.

The autumn season was in full swing, and the flowers

in the medians separating the two sides of the street still bloomed in wild, colorful profusion. The tree branches and leaves waved in the breeze, and it was already starting to get chilly.

I walked the half a block, feeling tired to my bones, from the emotionally exhausting day. I'd actually called Megan to cancel, but she'd sounded so happy we were meeting I didn't have the heart to let her down. But opening up to Max had left me feeling anxious, and I wanted to retreat into the safety of solitude that I knew so well.

Frankie's Fiesta had a bright red door, which opened as soon as I approached, and the host welcomed me. My eyes adjusted to the slight dimness, and I easily found Megan at the bar, sitting on a high backed stool. She hopped off when she spotted me, hurried across the floor, and enveloped me in a huge hug.

"Hi." I squeezed her back, surprised when some of the day's tension eased out of me.

Her eyes searched my face. "Uh-oh. You look tired. Everything okay?"

I opened my mouth to lie, but this was Megan, my

friend, and she looked so concerned. . . So, I blurted, "No, everything's awful. The inn needs *so* much work. We have a plan to get it in shape to put on the market, but it breaks my heart that we have to sell it. My grandma's will forces the sale, though, and it's so hard being there without her, you know?" I covered my mouth, feeling lame for unloading on her like that. "Sorry. I'm babbling."

"It's okay." Her hand rested on my shoulder, a familiar gesture that brought a lump to my throat. "I can't imagine how sad you must be about your grandma. I know how much you loved her."

"Thanks." I put a hand to my chest. "Now, please tell me they have margaritas here."

She giggled. "The best in the west! Paco, the bartender, knows how to make any kind you could possibly want. His red cactus margaritas are my fave."

We slid onto the barstools and ordered two red cactus margaritas from the waiter, along with an order of loaded nachos. Megan started chattering away and I soon found myself drawn in by the low lights, the soft music, and the extreme amount of tequila in the glass that had been put down in front of me.

"Do you remember how we used to pour soda into my mom's crystal flutes and pretend we were grownups sitting at a bar having drinks?" Megan asked.

I laughed, my mood lightening at the memory. "We were pretty goofy."

"I guess some things do come true." She tilted her glass toward mine, and we clinked them together.

"Didn't you say you might invite Olivia?" I asked.

Her expression changed. "I did invite her. But she's really busy, working on the Pumpkin Festival."

I sighed. Guess Olivia didn't want to be anywhere near me. Something I'd deduced from her attitude that morning. "She's mad. Isn't she? Give it to me straight."

"She's not mad." She twisted her mouth to the side. "But, she is hurt. Can you blame her, though?" Her voice went soft. "You kind of vanished on us. We never thought that would happen, since we were supposed to be best friends forever. Right?"

Her words stung. It also didn't go unnoticed that she'd used the term "we." Megan was hurt, too. Guilt washed over me. "I'm sorry. I never intended to just disappear, but I guess I did. I worked so hard to get my business off the ground, and that became my focus. I never meant to hurt anyone."

She fiddled with the stem of her glass.

"I think subconsciously I wanted to forget Blue Moon Bay, and put that part of my life behind me. You know how I felt about my parents leaving us, and there's something else I never told you." I slugged a huge gulp of margarita for courage. "Ian and I didn't just grow apart, and mutually decide to break up like I claimed. He cheated on me, then dumped me."

Her eyes narrowed. "I *knew* there was something slimy about him!"

My spirits were as low as the level of my glass, which was nearly empty. "I should've told you about Ian, but I was embarrassed. He obviously didn't want me. Story of my life."

"He was a moron." She put her hand on mine, and squeezed. "Your parents have issues that have nothing to do with you or Brian. You're both awesome. I know it doesn't get rid of the hurt, but *they* are the ones missing out by not having you guys in their life," she said, emphatically. "You're an amazing person, Wendy. Don't ever forget that."

I smiled at her through my tears, then inhaled deeply. "You're still my cheerleader."

"Always," she said.

I dabbed the corners of my eyes. "So Blue Moon Bay still has that Pumpkin Festival, huh?" I asked, trying to get things back on a more pleasant note.

"Oh yeah." Megan laughed. "That thing is still the highlight of the season, too."

The season. There were plenty of festivities that made tourists flock to Blue Moon Bay, no matter what time of year. Summer had always been the best time for the inn, although there were slower but still steady seasons.

"Do you remember all of the Pumpkin Festivals we went to growing up?" I lifted my drink again and drained it. The waiter reappeared, setting down our nachos, and I gestured for a glass of water. "We would run around on our sugar highs, flirting with boys." As soon as the words left my mouth, I pictured Max. His blue eyes, warm smile, sweet caresses. . . .

Megan giggled, unaware my mind had drifted. "I

remember when we got sick eating all those corn dogs and cotton candy that one year. We were scared to tell our parents, because we'd been saving our lunch money for a week in order to buy all of those forbidden goodies."

I smiled at my friend, fighting to push Max out of my mind. "Was it you or Olivia, who threw up on the merry-go-round that year?"

"Me." She sported a thumbs up sign. "Very classy. At least the concession stand money went to a good cause."

"Are they still donating all the proceeds to charity?" I asked.

"Yes, but now they choose a different charity every year. This time they're donating to a children's literacy program. They also change the theme of the games and stuff now, which makes planning a lot more work. When we were kids they used the same games every year."

"Yes, but I never got bored with them. I especially loved the game where you had to bust the balloons with darts to win a prize. My aim was always too far off to win, though."

"I still have the traditional glass whale, filled with the

clear blue liquid that they gave away as the prize for winning that game."

I propped my chin on my fist, taken back to my teenage years. "I'd always wanted to win one of those glass whales. I remember one year I cried so hard, because everyone had won one except me."

"You were upset? I never knew that."

I shrugged, remembering there was a lot I never felt comfortable telling my friends. "When my grandma saw how upset I was, she ordered one from the manufacturer, and gave it to me. I cried harder when I saw it, though, and told her it wasn't the same as winning one." I played with the tiny straw in my drink. "You know she never spent money unnecessarily. I realize now what a huge gesture that was for her. I should've appreciated her more."

She shook her head. "You were just a kid. We all do dumb things when we're young. Your grandma knew how much you loved her. And she loved you, too."

I pressed my lips together. "Thanks, Megan. I needed that."

She popped a loaded chip in her mouth. "So what

made you get into real estate?"

"I worked in a real estate office in college, and kind of caught the bug. I love touring houses, creating listings, finding people their perfect home. Maybe because I always wanted a permanent home of my own. . . I don't know. I love my work, and can't imagine doing anything else."

She swallowed another bite, then licked a glob of sour cream from her finger. "Okay, tell me the truth. Is being a Realtor as hard as it looks on television?"

"I didn't know it looked hard on TV." I tucked my hair behind my ear, and instantly thought of Max, and how he liked to tuck my hair. Sigh. Maybe I *should* just go on a date with him. Or maybe that was the margarita talking. Good thing I only ordered one.

Her eyes lit up. "It looks like so much work, but I love watching people try to find their perfect house. It's also entertaining when they put the Realtors through all kinds of wringers and stuff. Although, a lot of them seem staged if you ask me."

My mouth fell open. "How can you love a show that puts Realtors through the wringer?"

"I just do." She laughed, good-naturedly. "Olivia loves them, too."

Hearing Olivia's name made me sad, so I pushed the thought from my mind. "So what are you doing for a living? We've been so busy talking about me, I forgot to even ask."

"I'm a web designer. Just launched my own company, so it hasn't had time to take off, but I've had a few clients. I'm still working at the dress shop full-time to make rent, and I work on web design from my kitchen table. But it fills my creative outlet, and it's practical. So, I can see it going somewhere."

Web design? A figurative light bulb went off above my head. "The inn could use a website. I'd actually been thinking that earlier. Grandma was old-school, and never put the business online. It would make reservations easier, and would be a fantastic selling point for a prospective innkeeper. Do you know how to do all of that?"

She squealed. "Of course. Are you hiring me?"

"If you want the job," I said, thinking it was a fantastic idea. "Something simple, with clean lines, and offering the ability to book and pay online."

"I accept!" She rubbed her hands together. "When would you want to look at a rough site?"

"As soon as possible, and thank you for helping me out."

"No worries." Her gaze drifted over my shoulder, then her face fell. "Oh, no. There's Derek, the guy I've been dating. He's here with another woman. Yes, it definitely looks like a date."

I leaned back, eyeing the dark-haired man, with his arm around a tall blonde. "Were you two exclusive?"

"No, but I thought we might be eventually."

"I'm sorry," I said, seeing how bummed out she looked.

She shrugged. "Whatever. He was a little snobby anyway. Brian couldn't stand hearing about him. Are you dating anyone right now?"

"No," I said, but my mind replayed Max's kisses last night. "Well, there is this guy I met. His name is Max, and he's staying at the inn. I'm not really seeing him, but he asked me out . . ." I rubbed my forehead. "We kind of kissed on the beach last night. A lot. But I only allowed a fun fling, because I thought he was leaving in the morning. Now he's decided to stay at the inn all month long. It's a disaster."

Her eyes practically glowed. "You kissed him on the beach last night? Under the blue moon?" She wagged a finger. "You're tempting fate, Wendy. He must be pretty hot, huh?"

"Oh, stop," I said, embarrassed. "He's a really nice guy and, yes, smoking hot. But he's more than that. He's considerate and a gentleman. He has this dog he adopted. She's darling and he's so good to her. . . What is it?" I swiped my cheeks in case there was salsa on my face. "You're looking at me strangely."

"You've got it bad." She laughed, then checked her watch. Her face fell. "I didn't realize it was that late. I'm sorry, but I have to open the store early in the morning."

"I should get going, too," I said. It was funny because I'd planned on making this a short night, but I'd quickly lost track of time. It felt so natural and easy being with Megan. I really had missed her. We'd have to find a way to keep in touch once I moved back to Sacramento. "Thanks for getting me out tonight," I said, handing my credit card to the waiter. Megan started to protest, but I winked at her. "Business write-off."

"Aw. Thanks, Wendy. It was great to catch up with you. Thank you again for the job. I won't let you down. Let me brainstorm a little, then I'll run a few website ideas by you."

"That sounds great." I signed the check, and we walked outside. We hugged, then she went left and I went right. When I'd walked halfway down the block, I turned back around.

Megan had turned around as well. She waved and I waved back. Wearing a big grin, she raised her hand, putting her thumb to her ear, and her pinky toward her mouth in our old traditional sign for "call me." For a moment, it seemed like home here again. Then I felt a pang, realizing the only thing missing was Olivia turning to give me a wave, too.

Chapter Seven

The coffee pot at the inn probably worked, but I was leery of the antiquated machine, and didn't want to go near the huge tin can of grounds sitting next to it. Instant coffee was so *not* my thing. But I needed my morning coffee fix.

Thankfully, the drive into town was short, and beautiful. I'd forgotten to set my alarm last night, so I'd accidentally slept in until nine this morning, which was totally unheard of for me. I always got up bright and early, ready to get as much work done as possible. Blue Moon Bay was obviously having some kind of effect on me.

Bay Side Coffee was open, but less packed than yesterday, which was nice since I'd already slept a lot of my morning away. One of the harried baristas behind the counter waved at me. "Same as yesterday, hon?" she asked.

"Yes, please." I blinked, surprised she'd remembered me with the chaotic line yesterday.

"Wendy, right?"

"Yes . . ." I nodded, totally impressed. One of the perks of a small town, I supposed. Maybe she'd had all of the other patrons memorized already, so remembering my name was only one more. Still, I marveled at the woman's ability to multi-task well.

The barista wrote my name on two cups, which reminded me that, in addition to my latte, I'd ordered one for Brian yesterday. Maybe he'd actually get it this time. It's not like there was any point in avoiding the inn when Max would be there the entire month now. I still couldn't believe he'd changed his plans because of me. It was terribly romantic. Too bad we didn't live in the same city, because the mere thought of a long distance relationship made my stomach churn.

I paid for my order, then moved to the end of the counter to wait for my drink. Holding my paper bag of pastries under my arm, I stared down at the notepad I'd brought with me. My eyes trailed over the ever-growing list of things we needed to have done to sell the inn.

The line started growing longer, just as my order came up. I smiled at the second barista, then turned away from the counter too fast, because I almost ran right into a woman with a mane of wavy red locks. Olivia! I jerked backward. Thankfully, the tight lids on my cups kept my estranged friend from receiving a caffeine bath.

"Oh, it's you." She pursed her lips, and gave me a bland look that said she was still peeved at me. Time to rectify that.

I held my arms wide, a drink in each hand. "Sorry, Olivia. I didn't see you there."

She raised a brow, and twisted her lips to the side. "You haven't seen me in a long time, so that shouldn't come as such a surprise."

Wow. She was capable of delivering a serious zinger first thing in the morning. She hadn't even had her coffee yet. "Yeah, well . . ." My voice trailed off as I racked my brain for something nice to say that might please her. "How are your parents doing?"

She let out a loud sigh. "They've recently separated."

"What?" I asked, sure I must've heard her incorrectly. "How can that be? They were like . . . the *perfect* couple."

"Apparently not." Olivia reached the front of the line,

and she gave the barista a pointed look. "I need the biggest coffee you have. Give me an extra shot, too."

The barista gave me an odd look, nodded, and turned away. Since I'd put my foot so deep in my mouth, I tried to redeem myself by asking, "Whatever happened to that guy I heard you dated after college? I forget his name, but Brian said he rode a motorcycle . . ."

"Oh, him. Yeah, he cheated on me. But thanks for bringing up that painful memory."

Zero for two. Ouch! My face heated. If I stuck my foot any further in my mouth I was going to suffocate on shoe leather. Olivia leaned closer to the counter, which my back was against, effectively trapping me. The coffee heated my hands a bit too much, but surely Olivia would find fault with me if I asked for a sleeve. My goal was to get her to like me again, so I couldn't risk it.

She waved at the barista, and her elbow got dangerously close to my nose. "Is my coffee ready?" she asked, even though she'd just ordered.

The barista stuck a container of milk under the little wand thing, making the milk bubble. "I'll have it ready in just a sec, hon."

"Thanks. I'm late for my meeting."

"I hear you're working on the Pumpkin Festival," I blurted, before I thought about if it was another shoe-in-the-mouth response.

Olivia gave me a look that confirmed I'd blown it again. "I'm doing the best I can with what I've got, anyway. We're short-handed and we don't have a venue yet either. So we're holding meetings wherever we can. Today it's at the park, which should be nice and distracting."

"You know what? I'm happy to help if you really need an extra hand," I said, which revealed just how far I was willing to go to get in Olivia's good graces again. It's not like I actually had extra time for worthy causes with everything that was on my plate right now. "I'm here for a month, and you guys are even welcome to hold the meetings at the inn."

The sour expression on her face faded. "Really? Are you serious?"

"Totally." I juggled the coffee from hand to hand. So hot!

She smiled this time, her mouth stretching wide. "I'm

touched, Wendy. That would be fantastic!"

"Here's your coffee." The barista passed the cup to her over my shoulder. I held my breath, just waiting for it to scald my skin, so Olivia could yell, "Karma!" But she merely wrapped her hand around the cup, and moved the hot liquid safely away from me. Whew.

We stepped away from the counter, and I blew into the lip of the lid, hoping to cool the liquid down since my hands were still uncomfortably hot. She set her own coffee down, removed the lid, then dumped a ton of cream inside. She stirred the mixture, took a long swallow, and let out a happy sigh. "I really appreciate your offer to help with the Pumpkin Festival, Wendy. That means a lot to me."

"No problem. I'm really sorry to hear about your parents. I'm also sorry bringing them up and, you know, the other thing." I risked a sip of my coffee, which thankfully didn't burn my tongue. Ah, caffeine. I so needed that right now.

"Oh, that's okay." She waved a hand, and we moved toward the exit. "That guy was a long time ago. I just started dating this new guy, actually. I have a good feeling about him. But we're at that awkward stage, because we don't know each other very well. It sounds lame, but I wish I knew another couple, who wanted to double date with us. To take the pressure off finding conversation, you know?"

Huh. I never had a problem talking to Max. It was more a problem to *stop* talking to him. Olivia looked so happy and so sad at the same time about her new guy, and that pulled on my heartstrings. "I just met a guy, too. I'm sure he'd be up for a double date if you really want."

Olivia beamed. "Oh! You're *so* awesome. I'm really glad we ran into each other this morning. Let me give you my number, so we can plan a time."

Outside the coffee shop, she juggled her cup and her large phone, and managed to take down my number before we parted ways. Feeling like we had a real shot at rebuilding our friendship, I held her number to my chest as I walked to my car. Halfway down the block, I turned around, and then my chest filled. Olivia had turned around, too! She put her hand up, with her thumb to her ear, her pinky toward her mouth, and she winked at me.

I got into my car, elation soaring through me, since

Olivia seemed happy with me again. But the happiness quickly changed to tension. What had I been thinking suggesting a double date? I'd just told Max last night that he had no shot in the world with me, and I'd meant it. Now I had to ask *him* out on a double date, without him thinking I wanted a relationship.

Yeah, this wasn't going to be too hard or anything.

****

I got back to the inn, my mind tussling over the problem of having to ask Max out on the double date. He was sure to think I was interested in him when I asked him out, which I *so* was. But even if things were to go well between us, the problem still remained that we didn't live anywhere near each other. I'd learned the hard way that long distance wouldn't work out. Not going down that road again, no matter how tempting he was.

I strode into the inn's lobby, then promptly stopped and stared at the mess in front of me. Drop cloths covered the floors and there was blue painters' tape up all over the place. I blinked, wondering if the barista had spiked my coffee with something a little stronger than an espresso shot, because surely Brian hadn't done this much work all by himself in the time it had taken me to get my coffee.

My gaze shot to the corner of the room, where Max stood, spreading a drop cloth on the floor. His shirt had lifted a bit in the back, exposing the skin above his jeans. I imagined running my hand over his shirtless back, and shivered. The memory of the evening we'd shared on the beach resurfaced. His sweet words, his touch, his kisses. . . .

I shook my head to make those thoughts go away, which was hard. The man looked beyond hot today, wearing worn jeans that were faded in all the right places. Instead of throwing myself at Max like I had the urge to do, I handed my brother his cup of coffee. "What is Max doing with those drop cloths?"

He accepted the drink, with an appreciative look. "He's helping to prep the room for painting."

Duh. "I can see that. *Why* is he helping?"

He sipped the coffee. "This is good. Where's my bear claw?"

I handed him the pastry, and frowned. "Max Huntington is a guest of the inn. He has better things to do on his vacation than help us paint."

"Apparently not," he said, through a bite of his pastry.

"He's a guest, Brian," I repeated, pointing out the obvious.

He shrugged. "He saw me with the supplies this morning and offered to help. Grandma always said free labor was a terrible thing to waste."

I sighed. He had a point. But why was Max helping out when he could be off sailing in the bay? That made no sense.

Brian went back to work, with his latte in hand.

I downed the last few drops of my coffee, while I watched the two of them taping up the trim and baseboards. Max squatted down to work on some low spots, and my gaze automatically zeroed in on his backside. It should be illegal for a man to look that hot in old jeans.

I forced my eyes away, and sucked in a breath. I needed to ask Max for a favor, which felt oh-so-awkward. I waited until Brian moved across the room, then I strode over to Max. I gave him my best smile, but it felt forced. I'd never been good at asking for favors.

"Good morning, Max." I stood next to him, the toes of my black leather heels pointed toward his white sneakers.

He bent his head to the side, and grinned up at me, "Good morning, beautiful."

A zing of pleasure zipped through me. I cleared my throat to remind myself not to flirt with this sweet, gorgeous man. "You don't have to help Brian paint the inn you know."

"Yes, but I want to help you."

My brows quirked. "You mean you want to help Brian."

He shook his head. "You were feeling overwhelmed, so I thought you could use my help."

"Really? That's very sweet." My stomach warmed at his thoughtfulness, but I reminded myself that he'd be off doing business in Japan in a month, so I needed to keep things on the "friends only" level. "To thank you for your help, why don't I take you out to dinner? I'll bring another couple along, too. It will be fun."

He squinted up at me, then stood. "Are you asking me out on a double date?"

"No . . ." This was more awkward than I thought it might be, and I had thought it would be pretty awkward. I sighed. "Well, sort of. But you and I would just be going as friends."

"As friends," he repeated.

"Yes." I nodded, squeezing my empty coffee cup in my hand. "I ran into one of my oldest friends at the coffee shop just now. She wanted another couple to come out to dinner with her and this guy, and I sort of agreed to go. Would you like to come? Don't think of it as a date, though. More like a free meal with a friend, and her friend."

He lifted my chin. "It's a double date, Wendy. Admit it."

My skin tingled from his touch. "Not a *real* one. We'd just be going for fun, and as a favor for my friend since she's not really comfortable going out with this guy alone."

"Are you talking about Megan?" Brian interrupted, his brows coming together.

"No. Olivia. Do you have to be so nosy?" I glared at him, and he stuck a piece of tape right on the end of my nose. I swatted at him.

Brian ducked out of my reach. "So, you're trying to get back into Olivia's good graces." He threw Max a look. "Olivia's pretty mad at Wendy here."

"How could anyone be upset with Wendy?" Max asked, fingering a lock of my hair.

My fists balled. "She's not mad at me anymore. Not since I offered to help her with the Pumpkin Festival, and go on a double date with her."

Brian shook his head. "Wendy seems pretty desperate for this favor, Max. If I were you, I'd hold out for a homemade cheesecake. She makes dynamite cheesecakes."

My mouth dropped open. "You can't extort a cheesecake from me."

"No, but he can." Brian pointed at Max.

Max grinned. "That's an exciting prospect. But I won't do this favor for a cheesecake."

My stomach sank, at the thought of letting Olivia down, and, I realized, at not getting to spend the time with Max.

He tucked the strands behind my ear. "I will do this

favor for you, though. If you want to make me a cheesecake, then that would be a bonus. But you don't have to."

"You'll really do the double date with me?" I stepped forward, a huge weight lifting off my shoulders. I was so excited I could kiss him. Well, I wanted to. Instead, I retreated a step.

"Not sure you want to wear this all day." He chuckled, peeling the blue piece of tape off my nose that my annoying brother had put there.

I covered my nose with my hand. Oh, embarrassment.

"Let me know where and when for dinner?" He touched my nose in a playful way, then turned and went back to work, placing some tape over a light switch plate. Under his shirt, his smooth muscles flexed and moved in a very nice way that had my heart beating a little too fast.

The phone rang, causing my eyes to flare. I raised my palms. "I'm not answering that phone, Brian. I meant what I said."

He shrugged, then sauntered over to answer it. Max climbed up a stepladder, his thighs flexing a little as he did. The man was in great shape. Just looking at him made my heart beat a little too fast and my breath catch in my throat. Not good. Time for me to get to work. I needed to return a call about a bid on the exterior paint job.

"Thanks again for the favor, Max. We'll have a good time. I promise." I swiveled, my heels clicking against the hardwood floor as I headed for the stairs.

"Hey, Wendy?" He spoke over his shoulder, his gaze meeting mine. "Am I going to get a goodnight kiss at the end of our date?"

I swallowed. Oh, that sounded tempting, way too tempting. "This is just a friendly dinner, Max. Friends don't kiss each other."

"That's too bad." He winked at me, then turned to tape a spot on the crown molding. His jeans cupped his bottom and his arm muscles flexed. I bit my lip. It was totally not fair that he looked that good doing manual labor. Painting clothes should be lumpy and shapeless and ugly, not hot and tight enough to show off a great body.

My cell beeped in my purse, so I pulled it out, to check the message. "Olivia wants to know if Saturday night at eight works for us."

He nodded. "I don't have any other plans. I asked out this smart, caring, beautiful woman I met on the beach, but she shot me down."

I moved toward him. "Max—"

"Are you going to console me?" He hurried down the ladder, pulled me to him, then lay his head against my shoulder. "Because as my friend, I could use quite a bit of consoling."

"Max." I laughed, loving the feel of him against me. "I'll buy you dinner. Maybe make you a cheesecake. But that's all."

"Mmm." He buried his head in my neck, breathed in deeply, and pressed his lips to the spot just below my ear. Then he gazed down at me with a smile. "That's enough for now."

My head felt woozy from his one, light kiss. I swayed a little as I watched him climb back up the ladder. "I'll meet you in the lobby at seven-thirty tomorrow night," I said. I'd have to bury myself in work, and stay away from him until then. Otherwise, I'd very likely take him up on his offer to console him, which was all I could think about right now.

Chapter Eight

The next morning, with my Bay Side Coffee latte in hand, I taped two paint samples to the wall of the lobby and stared at them. One was a sea-foam blue, very near to the original paint color on the wall. The sea-foam blue was beautiful, and it brought a lump to my throat. Grandma had loved that color, and she'd had the inn's interior repainted twice with that color, while I was growing up. I could almost see her now, standing over the painters as they worked, her eyes sharp, making sure there were no runs or lumps in her paint.

The other color I'd whittled the choices down to was a lovely, shining beige. Using a light and bright color is an old Realtor and interior design trick. We use it because it works, making spaces seem larger and more open than they might be. Brian and Max had finished prepping late last night, after they'd scarfed down the pizza I'd ordered for them.

Max had thanked me for the pizza with a light kiss on the lips, assuring me that it was just a friendly kiss. The problem was I'd wanted more. Somehow I'd resisted, but I'd gone to bed dreaming of that one sweet, simple kiss. Every little kiss he gave me was magic.

I sipped my coffee and sighed, trying to focus on my real estate decision: sea-foam blue or beige. Which would Max think I should choose? Not that I would call him. He'd taken off for a run down the beach with Lucky earlier, and I hadn't seen him since.

Focus, Wendy. Paint colors. I had my cell in my hand, my index finger hovering over the screen. I tapped the address book and the paint store's number came up. I hoped that would help me make a decision, but the screen went blank again before I could.

So much for technology making my life easier.

"What are you doing, sis?" Brian walked up and peered at the paint samples. In addition to running the inn with Grandma, he was a handyman. So he knew what paint samples look like and he knew exactly what I was doing. But I placated him anyway. "I'm trying to decide between that beige and that blue."

He sipped his latte. "The blue, for sure. Grandma would have you weeding outside for days if she saw that boring ugly white."

I rolled my eyes. "It's *not* white. It's beige."

"It's ugly," he said, without hesitation.

"No, it isn't." I tilted my head, suddenly wondering if beige was ugly. Great. My brother had me questioning my Realtor eye, something my clients gave me a fat commission for since I knew what I was doing. "We should go with the beige. It's classic."

He stepped closer to the paint sample, until he was eyeing it from inches away. "Okay, it isn't run-screaming-with-your-eyes-exploding-ugly, but it's not the color the inn has always been either. I don't like it."

I looked at him. He had a roll of painter's tape in one hand, and his foot tapped quickly on the floor. I raised my brow. "Change can be a good thing you know."

"Not when it comes in beige." He plucked the beige sample off the wall.

I yanked it back from him, then taped it up firmly. "Stop messing with stuff. We shouldn't make the decision based on what you, or I, or Grandma would want. We need to choose what will make the inn sell well."

He shook his head. "Look how pretty the blue is. It looks almost like the current color, but it's not faded."

I tapped the phone into my palm, and surveyed the room. "Just think what this room would look like in this beige, though. The pictures would stand out more. The place would lighten up, and it would look—"

"Boring." He raised his cup to me, then knocked back the rest of his coffee.

There was no point in responding. I just needed to clear my head, and make a rational decision on which color would work better for the sale. I stepped back a few inches, then a few more. I closed one eye, then opened it again. The beige was the obvious choice. That little patch was clean, shimmery, and perfect. The image of Grandma waving her finger at me popped into my head, and I cringed. No, I had to leave emotion out of the equation, and order the beige. Decision made. I tapped the screen on my phone again, but did not hit the dial button.

The beige *was* perfect, but I loved the blue. Sigh.

Brian stepped back, until he was next to me. His shoulder jostled mine. "Admit it, sis. That beige does not look right in this inn."

"It's clean, neutral, and the smart choice. People don't always buy houses that have blue walls. In fact, it can be the kiss of death. I had a house in Sacramento that was gorgeous. It was huge, and the lot was impressive. I couldn't sell it, though, because the owners had painted the interior bright colors. Not everyone *likes* bright colors. It looked like the Easter Bunny had gone postal in there. The sellers wouldn't listen to anyone either. They refused to paint, because they loved the colors. It sat on the market for almost two years."

"But it did sell, right?" His head turned and his eyes met mine.

"Yes. But not until they relented, and repainted the interior. Guess what color?"

He raised his brows. "Sea-foam blue?"

"You're hopeless." I walked up to the wall again, tilting my head at different angles.

Brian gave me an odd look. "What are you doing?"

I blew out a breath. "Just trying to view the colors from all different perspectives. The freaking beige just doesn't look right in here for some reason."

My phone rang from my purse on the front desk. I

gave Brian an apologetic look, then strode over and pulled it out. I checked the number. It was my assistant, Janine. Uh-oh. I'd just talked to her twenty minutes ago, and asked her not to bother me until the afternoon unless it was urgent.

There had to be something wrong, and I just didn't need any more problems right now. Not when the image of Grandma wagging her finger was still haunting me.

****

I walked away from Brian, who was busy taking the beige sample down and sticking it to his forehead. I had no idea what he was hoping to prove with that gesture.

I answered my phone. "Hello?"

"Hi, Wendy. I'm sorry to bother you." Janine's voice came out rushed.

"What's up?" I asked, crossing fingers there wasn't a problem.

"We have a problem. A big one. Well, three."

I pressed the phone closer to my ear, and dropped my chin to my chest. "Tell me. What's going on?"

"You know how you asked Elizabeth to cover for you? Well, that's not working out so well."

"What? Why not? She has great sales skills, and she knows houses. Her dad was an architect and her mom is a designer. She knows values . . ." Okay, I was rambling. Talk about denial.

"The woman is going through a nasty divorce, and I think she's turned to the dark side." Janine paused, then groaned. "She worked with three of our clients this week. The first client, Reader, said he would stick a knitting needle in his ear before he went on another showing with her again. You'll recall his budget is one-point-five million?"

"Yes." My shoulders squeezed together, hoping Elizabeth hadn't let her personal life blow his business for us. "I'll call him, and see if I can smooth things over. What else?"

"The Obersts. They called me, wanting to pull their house from the MLS, because Elizabeth described their house as Neo-Gothic style in the listing."

"It *is* Neo-Gothic. Did you tell them Elizabeth consulted with a well-respected architect and designer before labeling the home this way?"

"Yes, but they didn't want to hear it. Mrs. Oberst

wants her home listed as traditional, but Elizabeth said she couldn't do that since, you know, it's Neo-Gothic."

I paced the floor, flexing the fingers on my free hand. "Elizabeth is right, Janine," I said, shuddering at what it would do to my reputation to list a home as traditional when it was totally Neo-Gothic.

"Lastly, there's Mr. O'Malley. In preparation for listing his house, he painted the interior pastel pink. Elizabeth warned him that it's unlikely to sell unless he changes the color, but he won't hear of it. Can you imagine someone purchasing a one-point-four million-dollar house with a pink interior? Mr. O'Malley doesn't even have a mortgage, but he says he can't move until his house sells."

"When he asked me what color to paint the interior I'd told him *beige*." That sentence made me turn my head to look back at the paint samples, one of which was currently stuck to Brian's forehead. I marched over to him and yanked it off then taped it back on the wall.

"Elizabeth just can't handle clients with the same finesse you do, Wendy. These three clients are threatening to withdraw their contracts from you."

"What?" I tilted my head, staring at the paint samples, wondering if Mr. O'Malley painted his house pink, because of a deceased grandparent's will that seemed just as strong from the great beyond as it had seemed in life. I pressed my fingers to my temple. "I'm sure Elizabeth can handle this, Janine. Don't you remember that client, who wanted three times what his house was worth? She got him to come down on his price, and the house sold in a week."

"I know, but that was before her divorce proceedings started. She's like a different person now. You have to come back, Wendy. We can't lose these clients."

Janine was right. These were big clients. My savings was being seriously depleted thanks to the major amount of cash I was pouring into the inn's makeover. The inn would sell, yes, but I'd have to wait until escrow closed before getting reimbursed.

Panic began to set in. I stopped walking. "I can't come back, Janine. I have to be here a month, and it hasn't been a full week yet. My family's depending on me, and they have to come first," I said, thinking of Brian and my grandma. I would *not* let them down.

She made an exasperated sound. "Can you come back for a day or two? Take care of these problems, then head back that way?"

"No, I need to be here one month. There's no way around it. I'll do my best over the phone to get them to give Elizabeth another chance. In addition to that, I need you to step up and be there in person with them as a buffer with Elizabeth. I know you can do that."

She took a deep breath. "Yes, I'll do my best."

An idea hit me. "Tell Elizabeth to show Reader Mr. O'Malley's pink house. Reader wants a good deal, and Mr. O'Malley needs to move. It could work out."

"But, it's pink!" Janine might have actually been hyperventilating.

"Yeah, but that's why she should tell him to bid well under the asking price. Have her reassure Reader that it's all about the layout, and that interior paint is a quick fix. Mr. O'Malley is asking well above market-price anyway. If Reader buys the house, that would solve two problems at once."

Janine sighed. "Okay. I'll keep you posted."

"Thanks." I hung up and walked back to the wall,

thinking of Mr. O'Malley. Why couldn't he have just painted the interior beige like I'd advised him. That made so much more sense financially.

The porch door opened and Max sauntered in, pressing his lips to my cheek. "What are you doing, beautiful?"

I glanced up into his baby blues, feeling the tension leak out of me. His hair was wet and I wondered if he had gone for an icy dip in the ocean. His arm bumped mine, and little flakes of sand fell to the floor near our feet. "I'm trying to decide which of these two colors we should use to paint the interior of the inn," I said, and found myself leaning into him.

He slipped his arm around my waist, squeezing me closer. "Which one do you like best?"

"I love the sea-foam blue." I gestured toward the walls, which surrounded us. The walls that I'd grown up in, that would soon belong to someone else. "The color looks like the paint that is already on the walls, though. I also love the beige, because the whole place would look clean and fresh, making the inn show better to a buyer. I'm torn."

His hand slipped around mine, his warm fingers closing over the top of my hand, and in between my fingers. Electric darts shot through my belly. I let myself sink into his hard and lean frame, until his warmth washed through me.

He lifted my hand, so our fingers were a bare inch from the samples. "Close your eyes," he said softly. "Stop thinking. Just go with your heart."

I took a long breath. He was too gorgeous, too sexy, and far too wonderful. I let my fingers stay in the air, breathing slowly and feeling his heat, his strength. My fingers came down on a sample, and it felt electric under my fingertips. I opened my eyes.

The sea-foam blue.

"Okay, blue it is," I said, and somehow the decision felt right.

With Max still holding me, I hit the screen on my phone, called the paint store, and ordered the sea-foam blue. I waited for my inner Realtor to scream at me for blowing this sale. Instead, the image of my grandma appeared in my mind. Her emerald-green eyes were as solemn as always, but the corners of her mouth curved upward, and she smiled at me.

Chapter Nine

I walked into the inn Saturday morning, holding a paper tray with four coffee drinks. I'd just gotten back from my morning ritual at Bay Side Coffee, where one of the baristas, Sandy, had greeted me by name. Next she asked me when the Inn at Blue Moon Bay would officially be listed for sale. I'd blinked in response, having forgotten that everyone knew everyone's business in a small town.

Instead of embracing the word-of-mouth advertising, as a Realtor should, I finally found myself saying, "We'll see," then I'd ordered four lattes, instead of two. Max had been working steadily with Brian, to prep the interior of the inn to be painted, so the least I could do was bring his morning caffeine. I also ordered a latte for Megan, since we had an appointment to view her initial website designs for the inn.

After the small talk at Bay Side Coffee, I thought about ordering a real espresso machine instead of going into town for coffee every morning. The clincher had been when Sandy tucked the cups into the holder, she'd said, "I hope you don't sell that beautiful inn to one of those tacky chain hotels that have been trying to get in here. I would die if I had to look at such a building every day."

That comment had left me feeling frazzled. Did I want to be responsible for the death of a really good barista? Or, for a decision that might adversely affect the people in town? Um, no. But would selling the inn really matter so much to the locals? I was afraid the answer was yes.

I strode across the inn's lobby, and spotted Brian and Max standing in opposite corners of the room, sanding the walls. Max's tee shirt clung to his strong upper body, and I took a deep breath, remembering what those muscles had felt like beneath my hands. Keeping things on the "friend" level with Max was getting harder every day. Plus, tonight would be our double date with Olivia and her new guy.

I'd barely handed Max and Brian their lattes when Megan sashayed through the double doors into the lobby. She'd swept her blonde hair to one side, secured with a rhinestone barrette. Her bright pink messenger bag swung near her hip as she walked.

"Morning, Megan." Brian gave her a wave. "I'd stop and talk, but I've been pressed into service. Manual labor. Don't let her get you, too."

She laughed. "Don't worry. I already set a fee."

"Good for you." He smiled.

I glanced back and forth between them, and decided I had to have imagined that little flirtatious exchange. After all, she was dating that guy from the yacht club. Or . . . I guess not anymore. I shrugged the thought off, because Megan having a romantic interest in my pain-in-the-booty brother was too disturbing. "Here's your latte. Why don't we work in the library?"

"Sounds good." Her gaze left Brian, and zoomed in on Max. She lifted a brow. I knew she'd probably deduced this was the guy I'd told her about, so I gestured between them. "Megan, this is Max. He's a guest at the inn, who has been helping us out with the renovations."

Max held his hand out. "Nice to meet you, Megan."

She took his hand, and gave it a little bounce. "I've heard a lot about you."

My face heated. I hoped he didn't think I'd gone into detail about our evening on the beach. Because I hadn't. Yet.

Max gave me a look that was filled with curiosity, so I quickly turned to Brian. "Have you seen the painters, who were supposed to start on the exterior today?"

Brian shook his head. "I'll give them a call."

"Great. I'll be in a meeting for awhile," I said, ushering Megan down the hallway and past the dining room. We sat on one of the sofas in the library, and set our lattes on the coffee table.

Megan whipped her laptop out of her pink bag, then took a long drink of her coffee. "We'll talk about domains and stuff like that today. I thought it would be best to do something really funky, and attention-grabbing for the website."

"This whole place is sort of funky and attention-grabbing already," I joked, sitting forward in my seat as I sipped my coffee. I stared at her screen. "I've never built a website before. The realty company had one built for me."

"Don't worry. That's what I'm here for. I secured

your domain name, and this is what I designed for your home page." She pressed a key on her laptop, then a photo of the inn appeared, the ocean providing a beautiful backdrop. "Hey, that's gorgeous. I love it."

She held a finger up. "But this is the best part. Watch."

I took a long sip of my latte, while I focused on the screen. The name of the inn appeared at the top of the screen one letter at a time. Then, seconds later, a giant whale jumped out of the water and ate the name of the inn. I choked on my coffee, gawking as the whale dove back into the ocean with a flip of its tail. A fake water splash hit the screen, the name of the inn reappeared, and Megan clapped her hands. "What do you think?"

I gaped at her, then back at the screen. She'd refreshed the page, and now the whale was, once again, gobbling down the name of the inn. Uh. . . I'd asked for a simple website, with clean lines, not something resembling a theme park ad! But she looked so excited. I had to think of a way to praise her work, while also explaining why it was not going to fly. I mean, hello? Whale?

"So, I love how creative and fresh the scene was. But I'm a little worried someone might wonder if they're going to get eaten by a whale if they book a room here."

She titled her head, and checked the screen again. "I hadn't thought about that. I have a few other ideas, though, if you would like to take a look."

Relief flooded through me. "That would be great."

"Okay, so how about this one?" She tapped a key on her laptop, and dolphins danced across the screen on their tails, holding bright blue beach balls with the inn's name on it. Oh, the horror!

My dreams of a very professional website crumbled right before my eyes. Why hadn't I remembered Megan's obsession with sea animals? She used to have pictures of them taped all over her room when we were kids.

Her lips pulled back into a teeth-revealing smile. "Don't you love it?"

I grimaced. It wasn't that I hated it, really. But it wasn't a professional site that would help me sell the inn. I set my cup down, and laced my fingers together. "The idea is fun and original, but I think it might be a little confusing for guests. I wouldn't want people thinking we had circus dolphins hanging around, and that a show option was available," I said, hoping my rejection hadn't hurt her feelings.

Her face was still as bright as ever. "If you don't love that idea, I have more."

The next sample site was a dark background, with a blue moon rising out of a steadily lightening sea. The words "The Inn at Blue Moon Bay" appeared on the screen, and beneath that, "Come experience the legend."

Megan pointed to the moon. "This is fun because it plays off the Kissed by the Bay legend. People come to Blue Moon Bay for romantic walks on the beach, to fall in love, or rekindle their romance. Right? What do you think?"

My mind shot back to when I met Max on the beach, by the bay, and our kiss under the blue moon. I had to admit, the site was romantic. "That's a clever use of the legend," I said, even though it was nothing like what I'd initially wanted.

She smiled. "Thanks. Why build a boring website like every other hotel? We should show what makes the Inn at Blue Moon Bay unique." She winked at me. "Plus,

I know the legend has a personal meaning for you. Max seems utterly dreamy. Tell me more about—"

My phone suddenly chirped, going off five times in a row. I glanced down to see the same text message from Janine over and over, which read: *EMERGENCY!!*

"It's my office. I'm sorry, but I have to take this. I'll be right back." I walked out of the room, then hurried down the hall, and dialed Janine.

"Thank goodness you called," she said, gasping into the phone.

My heart pounded. "What's going on?"

"It's your townhouse. The big one in that posh neighborhood you love so much, that's walking distance from the office."

"What about it?" I asked, my heart pounding in my chest. The owner had contacted me last month, to tell me they would be putting the home on the market soon. But he promised to let me know beforehand, so I could make the first offer.

"It just hit the open market."

My blood pressure shot up into the red zone. "That can't be the same property. Mr. Wells promised me I could put the first offer on that home."

"Yes, but they've separated. *Mrs. Wells* is the one who listed it!"

Oh, no! The townhome going on the market was supposed to be the best news ever. It was supposed to mean I'd finally purchase the stable home I'd always dreamed about. But I'd already used my savings as deposits for the roof repairs, the floor refinishing, the exterior painting, and so on. I wouldn't qualify for a mortgage without a down payment.

We had to sell the inn *now*, or I'd lose my perfect townhome. In terms of the will, escrow would put us over the thirty required days that I had to run the inn. But I hadn't listed the inn for sale yet, because I'd planned to give it the facelift first to entice an innkeeper who would keep our beloved inn running for decades to come. But would that decision cost me the home I'd always wanted? It didn't seem fair. I wanted to ask my grandma what to do, but she couldn't help me now. Nobody could.

"I'm really sorry, Wendy." Janine sounded as devastated as I was. "I thought you would want to know in case there was a way for you to buy it."

I swallowed the lump in my throat. "Thanks, Janine. I have to go now."

We hung up, and I squeezed the phone in my hand. I couldn't believe Mr. Wells had caved. That was the house of my dreams, and I'd worked so hard, giving up everything for it. I closed my eyes, envisioning the cool granite countertops, the long sunlit rooms, the park view of trees—which was a gem to find near downtown Sac— and my short walk to work. I couldn't let my home slip away from me. But what could I do?

With a heavy heart, I went back into the library. Megan was standing at the long windows when I returned. She gazed out at the view, overlooking the sweep of green lawn, and the beach just beyond. Out on the blue water, a sailboat bobbed, its sails filled with wind.

"It is so beautiful here. I wish my apartment had this view. What I would give to wake up to that sight every morning. You have no idea how lucky you are." She turned away from the window, saw my face and bit her lip. "What's wrong?"

I shook my head, and blurted, "I just found out my

dream house is on the market. I had a promise from the owner that I would be able to put a bid on it before anyone else, but they just listed it for sale. Someone could be putting an offer on it right now for all I know."

Her brows came together. "Sacramento is a big city. Don't they have other houses you would love?"

"Not like that one." I went back to the couch and pulled up the MLS, using Megan's laptop. My heart stopped when I found the listing. I gestured at the beautiful townhome. "Isn't it perfect? Look at the interior, too. See that soaker tub and those countertops? It's also the ideal location for long hours at the office."

"Um . . ."

My eyes bulged. "Does it say sold?" I stared at the screen, but all I saw was a glamour shot of the airy living room. "What is it, Megan?"

"Well, isn't it a little plain?"

"Clean lines are simple," I said defensively. I wanted to keep extolling its virtues but it was obvious she didn't like it. Her idea of a cool house would probably be one with Wyland murals on every wall, which was fine. That one suited her, and this one suited me.

"I'm sorry about your townhome, Wendy. Do we have a winner on your inn's website at least?"

Oh, great. I needed a good website now more than ever. Something clean and simple, just like the townhome I wanted. We had to get into escrow fast, though, on the offhand chance the townhome didn't sell out from under me. They had priced it a little high, although I would pay full asking price in a heartbeat. "I'll take the version with the romantic couple under the moon."

Megan beamed. "I knew the legend would be your favorite. You loved that story when we were kids. You always believed that was how you'd find your true love."

"That was before I was cheated on, and dumped." I pointed out. The legend did still hold a special place in the back of my heart, but all I could think about right now was my townhome. I needed to get the inn listed, and I needed a website. I tapped my finger against the coffee table. "How soon can you get it done?"

"It should only take a few days to get everything set up. I have an authorization form right here, and once you sign it I'll get to work right away." She pulled out the document, and I scanned the paragraphs, then signed on the line. As she stuffed it back into her bag, she asked, "Max is the double date guy Olivia told me about? Right?"

I ran a hand through my hair, feeling stressed beyond belief. In all of the commotion, I'd forgotten about my date with Max tonight. "He and I are just friends. We can't date for real, because . . . it's just too complicated."

"What's complicated about falling for someone? He seems nice, and you get all giddy around him like I've never seen you do before. It's pretty obvious he's crazy about you, too."

"He is nice, and I do like him," I admitted. "But after we sell the inn, I'll be back in Sacramento, and he'll be off for some project in Japan. If we don't live by each other, that makes any kind of relationship impossible. Long distance things never work out."

Her eyes became large and sad. "Why won't you consider staying in Blue Moon Bay, Wendy? Is it really so bad here?"

I thought about the reasons. My parents had abandoned me here, and it still hurt. Whenever I thought about Ian's betrayal, it felt like a knife to the gut. Even after all of these years, this town was still a painful reminder of the pathetic girl I used to be. "My life is in Sacramento, Megan. There's nothing here for me."

Max peeked his head through the doorway. "I'm sorry to interrupt the two of you, but I need to talk to you for a moment, Wendy."

His blue eyes darkened, and I sensed it was bad news. I wasn't sure I could take anymore today. My stomach sank. "Is there a problem?"

"I called the painters, and they got the dates wrong. They can't start until next weekend."

My mouth fell open. "But we're on a time crunch. Things have happened . . ."

"What things?" he asked.

I sank back into the sofa. "There must be a way for them to come out sooner."

"They scheduled another job, so it will have to be next week. Sorry, Wendy."

"Hey, Max?" Megan waved him over. "Check out the inn's new website design."

With one last concerned look at me, he bent over her computer, taking a quick peek. Then shot me a grin.

"That's incredible. I love how you've tied in the legend with the inn, which is an enticing feature here."

My gaze connected with his, and my belly fluttered, which was *not* good. I'd been trying to keep my emotional distance from Max, but each day pulled me closer to him. But now my townhome was on the market, and getting the inn listed for sale might be delayed. If only there were another legend. One that told me what I should do, when everything I wanted in the world was falling so far out of reach.

Chapter Ten

Max met me in the lobby at seven-thirty sharp. He wore khaki shorts that showed off his tanned, muscular legs, and a short-sleeved button-up shirt along with a pair of canvas deck shoes. He carried a light hoodie in one hand and I was relieved to see it. We were going sailing and it could get cool out on the bay. He smiled at me. "You look beautiful."

I'd pulled my hair back into a ponytail, and I wore a pastel blue long-sleeved shirt, a pair of denim capris, and deck shoes. It was a far cry from my usually formal attire, and his compliment eased my nerves. "You look great, too. I'm ready if you are. We're meeting Olivia and her date at the docks. It's just a couple minutes drive from here."

He took my hand and placed it in the crook of his arm in a gentlemanly gesture. A little bolt of electricity shot up my arm. I should move away, but the heat of his skin on mine, and the tantalizing scent of his cologne kept me tethered to him. We walked out of the inn, hopped into his rented convertible, then drove to the docks where the boats sat at anchor, their hulls rising with the slow swell of the waves below.

"Thank you again for doing this favor for me," I said. My nerves were raw, and I felt like a young girl on her first date, which was crazy. I already knew Max, and we'd already kissed (a lot). Plus, it wasn't a *real* date, so I had nothing to be nervous about. Maybe I should tell that to the butterflies who had taken up residence in my belly.

He flashed me his sexy grin. "You don't have to thank me for spending time with you, Wendy. It's what I've been wanting to do since the moment I met you."

"You're sweet." The butterflies fluttered wildly. He brushed his finger along my jawline, and the tingling I felt made me wonder if I was losing my mind. How could I stay "just friends" when everything about him made me want so much more?

Olivia waved from the top of the docks. She skipped over to us. "Hi, guys. I'm glad you're here. I was worried you might get hung up and not make it."

"I wouldn't let you down, sweetie." I gave her a hug,

warmed by the fact that she'd returned it with just as much enthusiasm. "Olivia, this is Max. Max, this is Olivia. She and I grew up together."

Max held his hand out. "Nice to meet you."

She smiled, shaking his hand. "You, too."

Olivia turned toward the man walking toward us. He had a full head of thick, blond hair, and light gray eyes that gave him a mysterious look. Olivia took his hand. "This is Hunter. Wendy, you remember him from elementary school, don't you?"

My forehead wrinkled. Did I know this mysteriously handsome man? Then it hit me. Hunter Cartwright! He'd been a skinny little boy, with a buzz cut, who had a strong fascination with ants. He used to follow Olivia down the halls at school, singing an off-key version of the Pink Panther theme song, inserting the words "dead ants" a lot. No wonder she was nervous. What if he decided to serenade her like during our grade-school days? Ha!

"Nice to see you again, Hunter." I held out my hand, and he squeezed it gently. Then he shook Max's hand as I introduced them.

We climbed aboard Hunter's sailboat. Max and Hunter started raising the sails, while I pulled Olivia off to one side. "Hunter sure looks different. But the way he looks at you says his crush seems to have lasted. Maybe we'll get a Cartwright version of the Pink Panther theme song tonight."

"Very funny." She nudged me with her elbow, then giggled. "I ran into him at a fundraiser I put together for my new business, but I almost didn't recognize him. He'd just arrived back in town after a high-powered job working on Wall Street."

Wall Street? That was impressive. "What is he doing back in Blue Moon Bay?"

"He's building sailboats now, like this one. That's always been his dream. He only went to New York to earn enough money to finance the business he really wanted. He leased a building, and has orders for five boats already."

"Wow." It sounded like Olivia had met the exact kind of guy I needed. A stable man with a long-term plan, who lived in the same town, and who would not abandon me to go flitting off to other countries. "Sounds like you and

Hunter might have serious potential."

"I think so, too." She gnawed at her bottom lip. "Megan told me you're interested in Max. But you guys aren't dating?"

I shook my head. "His job takes him all over the world. He doesn't live in Sacramento and he probably never would. If this turned into a relationship, that would mean I'd have to travel and give up my career, and I've worked too hard to do that. Plus, this would be far in the future, but what about when we had kids? All of the traveling wouldn't be fair to them. I'd never do to my kids what my parents did to Brian and me."

Instead of any kind of sympathetic look, she laughed. "You don't want to date him, but you're already thinking about what would be fair to your kids? Hate to break it to you, Wendy. But you're into him big time."

She was so right. I shouldn't be thinking about our future children when it was so obvious Max was *not* the man for me. Wanting to change the subject, I gestured toward Max and Hunter, who had already gotten the foresail up. "We should go help them."

I laced my arm through hers, guiding her over to the

sails. As teenagers, Olivia and I had sailed together many times before, and I knew she could hoist with the best of them. The matchmaker in me knew that Olivia was just being shy around Hunter, because she liked him so much. "Hunter? Why don't you let Olivia give you a hand with that line?"

Olivia retreated a step. "No, that's okay."

I grabbed the line, thinking she would take it. Instead, I tripped Hunter with it. He nearly fell, but, after an awkward movement, managed to stay on his feet. I dropped the line like it was a snake that had just bitten me. Oops.

Olivia dashed over to him. "I'm so sorry, Hunter. That was my fault."

"No worries." He touched her shoulder, and smiled.

I stood frozen, wondering what had just happened.

Max slipped his hand around me. "Want to help me with the jib?"

"Why don't we let Olivia and Hunter handle that?" I retreated away from him, because just that light touch, that amazing sweetness of his, made me want to grab him and kiss him. I retreated quickly, and backed into the boom, which swung forward. I watched in horror as it connected with Max's skull with a heavy thump.

My hands flew to my mouth. I'd just singlehandedly almost hospitalized half the crew of this boat. They were so going to kick me off this double date. "Are you okay? I'm *so* sorry."

He rubbed his head. "Don't worry, beautiful. I can still see just one of you."

I inhaled deeply, on the verge of a major freak out. "Olivia, why don't you and Hunter undo the line and pull the anchor, while Max and I get the jibs and foresail up?"

She looked at me like I was nuts. "I don't want to lean over and grab the line."

I blinked. Her shorts weren't tight and her neckline didn't look like it would gape to an embarrassing degree. I turned toward Hunter, but he stepped away from me like I had a contagious disease. "Well, why don't the guys do the jib, then Olivia and I will cast us off when you're ready?"

I didn't really care if they did the jib, or not. I just wanted to get the men out of earshot so I could find out what was going on with my jittery friend. "Olivia, what's wrong? Why don't you want to help with the boat?"

She hugged herself. "I-I almost drowned a few years ago, and guess I'm a little afraid still."

My mouth fell open. "Oh, Olivia. I didn't know . . ." Guilt rolled through me. Of course I hadn't known, because I hadn't been around. "I never should've pushed you to help. I was just trying to help you feel comfortable around Hunter."

Yeah, that plan had seriously backfired.

I came up next to her. "Why don't we let the guys handle the sailing stuff then?"

She rubbed her sides. "Yeah, let's do that. I'm not sure they can handle any more help from you anyway," she joked, then winked at me. "Do you know how to make a Bloody Mary?"

"Yes, that sounds like a safe job for me." I followed her into the little cabin, and we mixed up a pitcher of the drink. I went a little heavier on the vodka than I normally did since I had the feeling I was going to need it. "Didn't Hunter annoy you in elementary school?"

She plunked celery into four glasses, then added ice and a slice of lemon to each one. "Yes. That Pink Panther stalking thing drove me nuts. He seems to be over that now." She laughed. "What about you and Max? Do you still think you'll mess your kids up that badly?"

I gave the pitcher a brisk stir. "I can't date him, Olivia. Logically, it would never work out. But when I'm near him, I'm drawn to him in a way I can't explain."

"It's the legend. You kissed him under a blue moon."

My tummy fluttered. "You and I both know the legend isn't real. It's just a story. Now let's take these drinks up on the deck."

Her grin told me she knew I was changing the subject. But she let it go. Out on the deck, the guys had cast us adrift from the dock, and Hunter had set a steady course. They came over and we all took a seat as the wind blew through the sails, and we headed out into the lovely evening.

Max sipped his drink, looking out at the setting sun on the horizon. "Thank you for inviting me to be a part of this. I haven't been sailing since I was in the Netherlands."

Hunter made an approving sound. "That must have been a great sail. Where else have you sailed?"

Max took a long drink of his Bloody Mary. "I did a short sail through some fjords in Sweden last year. I travel a lot for work, but I try to fit a sail in when I can."

Hunter turned to me. "How about you, Wendy? Do you travel a lot?"

"When I was young," I said, a memory from my family's time in Brazil hitting me. It was right before we'd moved to Blue Moon Bay. My parents had friends who owned a boat, and they had taken the four of us sailing. We'd laughed so much together. It had been a wonderful day.

Max slipped his arm around me. "Traveling is fun, but there's no place like home."

Olivia picked up a cracker with cheese. "Is this your first time in Blue Moon Bay, Max?"

He shook his head. "No, my parents brought me here when I was a kid."

I'd been reaching for one of the crackers—a delectable-looking one with chutney and Brie—but my hand froze in mid-air. My gaze shot to his. "You've been here before?"

He nodded. "When I was twelve, my parents came to

the coast for a party at their friends' summer house. We stayed at the inn, along with several other families we knew."

I realized my hand was still hanging over the plate, so I brought it back to my lap. "You stayed at our inn? I don't remember you."

He chuckled. "Well, there were a lot of people there that weekend, so you probably never noticed me. Your grandmother sure did though. She gave me a real good lecture after she saw me jumping from my second story balcony into the pool."

A rush of tingles floated up my spine. No, it wasn't possible. Max couldn't be the boy I'd dreamed about all those years. The boy I'd thought about every time I heard the legend. I touched his hand, unable to believe what I was hearing. "That boy was you?"

"Yes . . ." He squinted, seeming to get from my expression that I'd noticed him, too. The corner of his mouth hitched up, and an electric energy coursed between us, tugging us closer together.

I stared into those beautiful blue eyes, but I was stunned speechless.

Olivia spoke first, "Do you know there have been signs all over the inn, ever since that incident, warning guests that jumping off the balconies is strictly prohibited? Every year, Wendy claimed she wanted to try it, but she was too scared her grandma would freak out if she did. We heard she really gave it to you after that stunt."

Max snatched a few grapes off the platter. "Did she ever. It only took her about three seconds to realize my folks were too busy to bother with me, and she took me under her wing, so to speak. She made me trim the hedges, and said the lesson would do me good."

I nibbled on a cracker. "Why would you take orders from an innkeeper when your parents were paying a premium to stay there?"

The corner of his mouth lifted. "I was trying to impress this girl, who lived at the inn. She seemed to adore her grandma, so I tried to take my punishment like a champ."

Tingles shot through me from every direction. The boy at the inn—*Max*—had noticed me, too? My heart thumped against my ribcage. This was incredible.

Olivia turned to me, smiling. "Are you impressed yet, Wendy?"

Hunter laughed. "Wow. I thought singing under Olivia's window, until her neighbors threatened to call the cops was romantic."

We all laughed, but I was still processing what Max had revealed. When he laced his fingers through mine, I didn't pull away.

I looked at Hunter. "You sang under Olivia's windows? I didn't hear about that."

Hunter finished off his drink, and set the empty glass down. "Well, I tried to, but she lived on the ground floor, and one of her neighbors tossed a pot of water onto my head." He stood and held out his hand. "Olivia, would you like to help me? I want to start tacking to the west."

She bit her lip, and took a long breath. I made a frantic little flapping motion with one hand, and she laughed. "Yes, of course," she said, as Hunter helped her out of the chair and they headed toward the boom.

I turned to Max. He sat sprawled out in the chair next to me, his bare knee touching mine, sending a rush of heat through my skin. "I can't believe that was you at our inn. I was impressed when you jumped off that balcony. You had this zest for life, which I envied. And you were incredibly cute." My gaze traveled over his handsome face. He was even more handsome now. "Your parents were furious when they found out what my grandma had made you do."

"Yes, they were. She was the first person who had ever talked to me about responsibility, though. My parents had raised me to think we were above the rules, because we had money. Most people were too afraid of making my parents mad, or losing their business, to treat me like a kid. It was a refreshing change, and your grandma taught me a lesson I never forgot."

I studied my hands a moment, before lifting my lashes, and a piece of hair fell against my cheek. "Were you really trying to impress me, Max?"

He tucked the piece of hair behind my ear. "I'm still trying to impress you. I think your grandma would be proud of the work I've done on the inn. Don't you think?"

"She would've loved you," I whispered, then leaned across the little distance between us, until our mouths met. As we glided along the water, my eyes drifted closed. His warm, soft lips parted, and his tongue met mine in a long and slow kiss that seared my senses. He tasted of cheese and drink, each stroke of his tongue sending ripples through my belly.

I never wanted this moment to end.

The boy I'd always dreamed about had become the man I'd tried to stay away from, and the irony wasn't lost on me. There was no more denying I'd fallen hard for Max, though. Since that day when we were twelve, he'd stolen my heart. I didn't know what to do about that, so I continued to kiss him, while the wind whipped all around us.

Chapter Eleven

The next morning, I woke up to the sound of the waves pounding against the shore outside my window. I cracked open one eye, glanced at my clock, and my eyes bulged. It was past ten in the morning already. I wanted to crawl under my pillow and keep dreaming of Max, but I rolled out of bed, and put my feet on the floor. I stood and stretched, trying to get some blood flowing into my muscles.

We had stayed out way too late last night, but the evening had been absolutely amazing: the long smooth sail along the shore, reconnecting with Olivia, and kissing Max—that had been *really* good. So good that we'd returned to the inn, soaked in the hot tub, and kissed some more. My lips were actually swollen from all of our kisses, but once I'd started, I couldn't stop myself. His kisses were addictive, and delicious—just like how I felt about him.

I took a quick shower, put on a pants suit, and headed downstairs, wishing I'd bought a new espresso machine already. I was mentally preparing myself for the drive into town as I walked into the lobby, but Brian met me and handed me a tall cup that had the delicious aroma of freshly roasted brew rising from it.

"You are so my favorite person right now," I said, taking the cup, and drinking the hot, delicious liquid. I'd never been so tired in my life. Or, so happy.

Brian chuckled. "I thought you might want to skip the trip into town this morning since you got in so late. That must have been some date."

"Mmhmm." I pried off the lid and blew on the steaming dark liquid, so I could down enough to wake myself up.

Brian watched me with interest. "So, how did it go?"

"We sailed along the shore. It was gorgeous."

He tapped his foot, and crossed his arms. "Not the boat. I meant the forbidden date with the inn guest, you know, with Max."

I knew exactly what he meant, but I didn't want to talk about it. The evening had been wonderful, like something out of a fairytale—or a coastal legend, as the case may be—but that didn't change the fact that there was no chance of us working out. But I didn't want to think about that right now. So I walked over to the table against the wall, and began flipping through the old-fashioned guest book, searching for the signatures from when I was twelve. The pages had gilt on the edges and the smell of the book stirred up good memories, making me smile.

Brian nudged my ribs. "If you don't want to talk about the date, then it must have been phenomenal."

"Hmm," I said, being non-committal. I tried hard to ignore my brother, but ignoring Brian was like ignoring a tsunami. Sadly, the guest book ended ten years ago. "Do you know where Grandma keeps the old guest books?"

"Not sure." Brian grinned at me, leaning onto the table. "Come on, sis. Spill it. Give me all the details."

I opened my mouth to answer, just as the door to the inn opened, and a couple marched in. I turned toward the pair, happy to be saved from my brother's nosy questioning. The man and the woman wore clothes that screamed money. The tall blonde woman had impeccably groomed nails and hair, and gave me a winning smile as they crossed the lobby together.

Brian stepped forward. "Are you checking in?"

She shook her head. "We're looking for the owner."

"I'm Wendy Watts, the owner." I extended a hand, purposefully not introducing Brian as an owner since she must be selling something, and I could handle her myself.

She took my hand, and gave it a hard pump. "Hello, Ms. Watts. I'm Louise Totsky and this is my husband Leon. We would love to take a tour of your inn."

"Are you interested in booking a room?" Brian asked.

"No." She shook her head, reached into her designer purse, and handed me a business card. "We heard the inn is going up for sale, and we're entertaining the possibility of purchasing it."

Adrenaline coursed through me. Could they really be serious buyers? My mind immediately raced with the possibilities. If they purchased immediately, and we had a short escrow, then I might be able to purchase my townhouse! Inside I was reeling, but I kept my face blank. "Well, it's very nice to meet you both." I straightened, holding my head high, incredibly glad I'd put on a suit this morning. "As you can see, the whole place is undergoing renovations. All cosmetic, a fresh facelift if you will."

"Wonderful." Her smile widened. "That would be less work for us."

Suddenly, I had a crazy hallucination. I pictured myself slamming the guestbook shut and flapping my hands at them, shouting, "The inn's not for sale! Move along, please! Move along, now!"

I blinked a few times, then took a quick peek at the book. To my relief it was still open, and Louise was still smiling. Weird. I blamed the Bloody Marys from the night before, but the feeling I had wouldn't go away. Something inside me didn't want to sell the inn to them. But that made no sense. I knew when a buyer was serious, that was part of being a good Realtor, and these two seemed serious. They could be the answer to all of my problems. So what was wrong with me? Ignoring my gut reaction, I said, "I'd be happy to give you a tour right now if you'd like."

"Thank you so much." Louise removed a camera from her purse and handed it to Leon, who began snapping pictures.

I set my coffee cup on the table, holding my hands

wide. "This is the main lobby, of course. The crown molding is original, and that window is being replaced. The floors are all hardwood, and we're refinishing them next week. The views are some of the most incredible in Blue Moon Bay, and are visible from all of the many windows throughout the buildings. Upstairs is the section with the bedrooms we keep for our personal use. Are you planning to live at the inn?" I asked, a knot forming in my stomach.

"Yes." She smiled tightly, glancing at her husband. "This seems like the perfect opportunity for us. We come from the city, but we're ready to have a slower paced life now."

"Have you been to Blue Moon Bay before?" I asked, as we walked through the hall, toward the attached buildings.

Louise shook her head. "No. We just came down a few days ago to visit a friend and we fell in love with the town. We're selling our business in San Francisco to get out of the city, and we're looking for a new adventure."

We approached the next building, and my brain went into overdrive. Maybe they didn't have the money right now. Maybe the purchase of the inn would depend on the sale of their business. I cleared my throat. "Are you planning to have a contingency on any potential offer? In regards to the sale of your current business?"

Her mouth curved into a smile. "No, any offer would be all cash."

My heart sank. I had no idea why. For some reason, part of me had been hoping she wouldn't say no, which made no sense. I'd taken a ring of keys from the desk and I used one to open an empty guest room.

Louise sailed in ahead of us. "Look at the lovely bay view. Just magnificent."

"Indescribable," Leon said, enthusiastically. "I like the whole idea of running the inn, living here, and seeing that view every morning and night. It's a perfect slice of heaven."

I bit my lip. "Do you have a timetable for when you would want to take the inn over, if you decided to purchase?"

"Since the sale of our current business will be handled by our lawyer, we could take over as soon as escrow closed," Louise said, without taking her gaze away from the ocean view. She gestured to her husband, who started snapping photos of the bay.

I bit my lip, irritated at their fascination with the view, and feeling like they were intruding on my private property. "We're looking for a buyer who plans to run the inn long-term."

"That won't be a problem." Louise gazed up and down the shore, before she turned back to me with a smile. "That's exactly what we plan to do."

"Perfect," I said, wondering about the gaping hole I felt in my chest. They did sound like the ideal buyers, so I should've been jumping for joy. Only I wasn't. Not even close.

I finished showing them the property, then we circled back to the lobby. I gave them my business card. They promised to be in touch soon, then they left the same way they came in, at full march. I sagged against the desk, staring after them. It might happen. They might buy our beloved inn. If things happened fast, I could make a contingency offer on the townhouse I wanted, too. I closed my eyes, seeing the automatic blinds, the sweeping balcony, the granite countertops, and hardwood floors. Everything was falling into place.

"What did they say?" Brian asked, his voice gruff.

My eyes snapped open. He stood near the desk, his arms crossed over his chest and a petulant expression on his face. I inhaled deeply. "They're interested buyers. I think they'll make an offer. I gave them a high asking price, and they didn't even flinch. She said any offer will be all cash, and they would want a short escrow. We'll make sure escrow closes after the will's thirty-day requirement ends, of course."

He scowled at me. "Then I'll have to leave my home."

I sighed and picked up my coffee, drinking a long gulp of it to soothe my throat and nerves. It didn't work, so I set it back down, and flicked my gaze to my brother. "This has always been the plan. The will says we have to sell the inn."

"Then you'll leave again, too."

My chest tightened. "I have to get back to my business. It's hard to manage it over the phone, and there's a townhome I'm going to make an offer on."

"So that's it?" He threw his hands up and stormed

out.

My phone rang, and I glanced at the San Francisco area code. "This is Wendy Watts."

"Hello, Wendy. This is Louise Totsky. I wanted to let you know my husband and I were pleased with the inn. We'll be submitting an offer shortly, and I hope you'll find it acceptable."

I tried to swallow the boulder creeping up my throat. "Thank you for letting me know. I look forward to receiving the documents."

I hung up and blew out a long breath. I should've been overjoyed right now. The inn was being sold way ahead of schedule, and the Totskys didn't even care if I finished the facelift on it, so maybe we'd save some money. The house in Sacramento was within my grasp now.

The look on Brian's face broke my heart, though. And selling the inn meant going back to Sacramento, where there would be no Max. No more moonlight kisses, and no more electric little tingles every time he touched me.

****

The Pumpkin Festival meeting was in half an hour and I needed to rush to get things done but I kept stalling. I wanted to talk to Max, badly. I wanted to tell him about my potential buyers and the house in Sacramento. I wanted to tell him everything about my day, but I hadn't seen him all afternoon.

I'd seen him heading to his room hours ago, so maybe he was still up there. I could go knock on his door. Or I could get things ready for the Pumpkin Festival. Or I could go talk to him, and *then* get things ready. The last idea sounded like the better plan, so I headed toward his room, a smile on my face at the thought of seeing him.

I knocked and heard footsteps, but I also heard him talking as he got closer to the door. I made out the words, "I know you need me there Monday, but I'm tied up here. Yes, I know how important it is to you. I'm sorry you feel that way." He let out a loud sigh. "I'll think about it and get back to you."

My heart twisted in my chest, and my smile dropped off my face. The door opened, and suddenly Max's blue eyes were peering at me. He pulled me into his room, and lifted me into his arms. Wrapping my arms around his neck, I settled in there as if I had always been there. I laid against his chest, my body melded to his, and I never wanted to move again. But then I remembered his phone conversation.

I leaned back, and he gave me a kiss that left me breathless. But it couldn't make me forget what I had just overheard. "Is everything okay?" I asked.

His answer was another kiss, and I sank into him. He squeezed my waist, before his hands traveled up my sides, past my shoulders, and finally cupped my face, as he held my mouth captive with his. When he pulled away, he rested his forehead against mine. "Everything's fine. My dad's just upset about the project I refused. Now he's demanding I fly to Tokyo on Monday for the project we already signed."

My heart didn't just sink. It plummeted all the way into my belly. I knew this would happen eventually. Max's family ran one of the most successful companies in the world, and of course they would never allow him even a month off. "Tokyo?"

He nodded, wearing a smile that broke my heart. "Have you ever been?"

It was obvious how much he loved traveling. I stepped back a little but not enough to leave his embrace. "Yes, when I was little. I don't remember much about it except that I was scared of the trains, and Brian wanted to ride the roller coaster but he was too little."

Max chuckled. "Everyone is afraid of the trains in Tokyo. They're terrifyingly fast."

My heart managed to drop a little lower. I knew that this time with Max had always been temporary, but I'd let him in anyway, and now he was leaving. I didn't want him to go, so I decided to change the subject. "Guess what happened today?"

"You fell through that bad section of flooring in the upper hall of building three?"

I laughed at that. Max had nearly gone through the floor the day before, and while it had been scary, and distressing, he had made it funny, too. Max had managed to make everything seem fun, but who was going to make me laugh once he left?

I shook my head. "No. We had potential buyers come in, and take a tour of the inn."

His eyes darkened. "How could you have buyers?

The inn isn't even on the market."

"They must've heard through word of mouth. Small town and all of that. They seem interested in living here and keeping the inn running, which was what Brian and I wanted. I'd worried I might get a flipper in here, or a developer that would want to tear the inn down, but they seem determined to run it," I said, giving him the high price I'd quoted them. "They didn't waver at the number, and called shortly after they left to say they're sending over an all cash offer."

His hands dropped away from my face, and his brows came together. "Are you sure about this, Wendy? Selling I mean? I'm just asking because you seem to love it here."

"Of course I'm sure." As soon as the words came out, my eyes watered, and I knew I wasn't sure. "I thought you would be happy for me. Now I can buy that townhouse in Sacramento I've always wanted, and I can go back to my business."

He set his phone down and petted Lucky, who was lying quietly on the foot of the bed. I knew I should tell him dogs did not belong on the bed, but I had a feeling she had been planted there for awhile anyway. He sat me down next to him, and lifted my hand. "I know you love the townhouse in Sacramento, but I think you love the inn, too. I never thought you'd really go through with it."

I sighed, pushing the hair away from my face. "Max, it isn't that simple. I live in Sacramento. Just like you live in San Francisco."

He shook his head. "I have a condo in San Francisco, but I've never really lived anywhere before. I just stayed there. I've only recently learned the difference." He squeezed my hand. "This town is home for me."

Shock rolled through me. "What are you talking about? You're leaving on Monday. You have the traveling bug just like my parents do."

"You're wrong. I love to travel, but this place is home for me. I feel it in my bones. No matter where I go, this will always be home. I will always come back here."

"If you're thinking of moving, then why not Sacramento?" I held my breath, wondering if I had just assumed too much. After all, this could just be a vacation fling to him. No, I knew that was my insecurity talking. He'd always been honest about his feelings for me.

"I could live in Sacramento for you, but it would never be my home."

I stomped over to the window. Outside the manicured green grass sloped down to the steps. The ocean lay in a great shimmering sheet of blue below. The sound of the waves came through the open window, and I placed my hands against the screen, feeling the heat of the sun beyond them leaching into my skin.

"Tell me you won't miss that." Max's breath washed over my shoulder and the heat of his body against my back made me lean against him, even though I wanted nothing more than to walk away before things got more confusing.

"You don't understand." My voice was barely a whisper as my throat tightened, and a hot tear escaped down my cheek. "Of course, I'd miss this place. I'd miss the sound of the water rushing against the sand, joking with Brian, hanging with Megan and Olivia, the memories of my grandma throughout the inn, and even the baristas at Bay Side Coffee. Most of all, though, . . . I'd miss you," I said, my throat closing up.

I'd let him into my heart, and now he was embedded

there, for better or worse. I turned around, and his face was close to mine. I tilted my head back, and he planted gentle kisses on both of my cheeks, before his mouth met mine in a sweet and fierce kiss, that left my senses reeling. His tongue melted with mine, over and over, his hands sliding up and down my back, until he pulled me tight against him.

Finally, I leaned back, fighting to catch my breath as hot tears ran down my cheeks. He wiped the tears away with this thumbs. "What's wrong, beautiful? Did you change your mind about selling the inn?"

I shook my head. "You talked about where home is, and I thought mine was in Sacramento. Now I'm not sure. But I have to go get things ready for the Pumpkin Festival meeting," I said in a breathy whisper. "I have people coming." I gave him a quick kiss and left his room, closing the door firmly behind me.

The Pumpkin Festival was in four weeks. With the way things were unraveling quickly, maybe I would be gone before the festival. If so, I would miss the cakewalk and the kids in the bouncy houses. I wouldn't get to throw darts at the balloons again, or get to see Max toss rings at the bowling pins, in order to win a goofy prize.

Everything was finally turning out the way I thought I'd wanted. We were most likely selling the inn, possibly for full price, and I had a good chance of getting my townhouse. I'd be able to get back to my real estate business a lot sooner than I had even planned, too. If everything was falling into place, then why was my heart breaking right now?

Chapter Twelve

I left Max's room and headed for the lobby. I got there just in time to greet Olivia and the other four women who were working to bring the Pumpkin Festival to life. Olivia introduced me to the others: Wren, a lovely older woman with silver hair and a slender figure; Erin, an energetic woman about my age; Tricia, another woman with a bright smile and a tan that made me instantly envious; and Suzie, who looked like she was in her late twenties and had an air of authority about her that I instantly liked.

We all shook hands and I led them into the library, where I'd arranged a table with bottles of water and snacks arranged on pretty plates. Tricia immediately went to the windows, peered out and exclaimed. "Look at that amazing view, girls."

They all gathered at the windows. Suzie used her hand as a sun visor, and said, "I can't believe how gorgeous that is. I've never been inside the inn before.

The whole place is stunning. I'll have to get my boyfriend to bring me here for a weekend getaway."

"It would make a charming staycation spot," Erin said. "Do you give discounts to locals?"

I shuffled my feet a bit. "I'm not sure if the new owners will offer a discount or not."

All of their faces registered surprise. Suzie asked, "You're selling this place? Why? It's beautiful, and a landmark too."

Olivia seemed to notice the downcast expression on my face, and cleared her throat. "Enough small talk, ladies. We need to get to business." She took a seat at the table and opened the file she'd had stashed in her large tote bag. I breathed a sigh of relief. It's not like I wanted to explain to perfect strangers that now that I'd fallen in love with the inn again, I had to sell it.

Olivia tapped her pen against the table. "I know that we all like the dunking booth . . ."

The others gave out a collective groan and Suzie shook her head. "No, not all of us."

"You don't?" I asked, unable to help inserting my opinion, even though I was a newbie. I sat down and put a lemon tart from the bakery onto my plate. "Why not? The dunking booth has always been there. It's a part of the festival, and a landmark in its own right."

"It's so boring, though." Tricia said, scraping the cream cheese off her slice of carrot cake.

I stared at her. "The dunking booth is boring? Not for the person sitting there. You never know when you're going to get dropped into freezing cold ocean water." I turned to Olivia. "Do you remember when we got talked into working the dunking booth? That was the year that major league baseball player volunteered as a celebrity dunkee?"

"Do I?" Olivia shook her head. "My hands looked like raisins for a week. I pretended to check the water like a zillion times just to be close to that hottie. I even volunteered to get dunked, in order to impress him."

"Me, too." I laughed. "It was fun, though. Wasn't it? Not boring at all." I could almost feel that hard seat below my bottom, and see the people lined up waiting for their turn to dunk me. Even being dunked had been fun. It was a lot like the way I'd fallen for Max. I'd barely taken one breath, and then . . . *bam* . . . I'd been plunged in all the way.

Tricia spoke, shattering my thoughts. "I think we should do away with all the hokey little things we've done in the past, and try new things. I hate the cakewalk, and the pie-eating contest. Besides, we're probably just promoting childhood obesity with those things. And the dunk tank is not something people want to do anymore. It's too big of a commitment."

"It's a dunk tank, not a marriage proposal," Olivia joked.

Erin raised her hand. "Tricia means we have to pay the deposit now if we want to reserve the booth, which means we have to make sure to collect enough money from the game to pay off the rental, and lately that has not been happening."

Who cared about money when we were talking about the dunk tank? It may be quirky and silly, but it had been a huge part of our life growing up. I couldn't imagine the Pumpkin Festival without that dunk tank there.

Could I imagine a life without the inn in it? I had left town, yes. But the inn had always been here. When I left this time, that wouldn't be the case. There would be new owners, and nothing would ever be the same. I could never drive through the gate, down to the circular drive, and know that I was almost home.

Wait . . . home? Had I just thought of the inn as my home? I needed to lay off the tarts. Maybe the sugar was affecting my brain. My home would hopefully be that gorgeous townhome in the city. Blue Moon Bay wasn't my home, anymore.

Olivia rapped her fingers on the table. "So, you don't want cake or pies or a dunk tank? None of the old stuff. What *do* you want then?"

Tricia clapped her hands. "I think we should ditch the petting zoo, and bring in some musical acts."

"Fun idea!" Suzie enthused as she forked a little key lime tart from the tray, and bit into it. For someone who was against pies and cakes, she sure seemed to enjoy the tart.

Olivia stared at them both. "Come on, guys. The kids love the petting zoo. I don't think it's a good idea to revamp the entire festival."

Tricia shrugged. "That's really the whole point, though. It's time to get rid of the old, and bring in the new."

I guzzled a long swallow of water. They could have been discussing my life, and not just the festival. Old versus new. Which was better? My gaze flew to the windows. The ocean lay just below in a perfect, smooth expanse that touched the far end of the horizon. How had I not craved that view, while I'd lived in Sacramento? Because I'd gotten rid of the old, and brought in the new. Huh.

"A musical act doesn't sound bad," Olivia said, jotting notes down on the paper. "Couldn't we have both? The petting zoo and music? A combination of the old and the new?"

Suzie tapped her chin. "I'd have to crunch the numbers."

Erin brightened. "We could use local talent."

"Good idea." Olivia scribbled a few more notes. "Now I'd still like to have the sack races . . ."

More groans.

"That is beyond tired, so let's get rid of that this year," Suzie said.

Tired? The sack races were a blast! Olivia, Megan,

Charlie, and I had competed every year in those races, usually tied to one another. Max had told me he was looking forward to the sack races, and he'd even suggested we race together. The idea of being tied to the ankle with him, and bouncing along in a burlap sack was most appealing.

Olivia laid her pen down and leaned across the table. "The sack races stay. They are cheap to do and everyone loves them, especially the tourists."

Erin set down her water bottle. "We'll put it to a vote at the end."

Olivia clicked the end of her pen repeatedly, which made sharp noises that echoed slightly. I knew she was annoyed, and I didn't blame her. The others were turning our Pumpkin Festival into something else entirely. Then it hit me. It wasn't *our* Pumpkin Festival. It belonged to Blue Moon Bay, and I didn't. I belonged in Sacramento. At least I'd always thought I did.

Blue Moon Bay would never have the excitement of Sacramento, or the opportunities I found there. Here, I'd never be the Realtor of the Month. Or, if I were, then it would hardly be such an accomplishment since there were only a handful of other Realtors in town. Why was I even debating between Blue Moon Bay and Sacramento, though? It wasn't like I even had a choice in the matter, thanks to my grandma's will.

"Before we vote on the activities, I'd like to make a speech," Olivia said. "Just because the dunk tank was a failure in the past doesn't mean it will be in the future. Things change. Maybe the only reason the game stopped working was because people didn't realize how much they loved it. We should give them a chance to love it again."

I totally knew what she was talking about. Blue Moon Bay hadn't worked for me in the past, and I'd forgotten how much I loved it. But thanks to my grandma's will, I had gotten another chance to love this town, and I didn't want to lose it again.

The vote for the dunking booth came and it was spilt right in half, two wanted to keep the game, and two didn't. I was the deciding vote. Olivia turned to me. "Wendy, we need a tie breaker. What do you vote?"

Stay or go? It wasn't just the dunking booth I would be voting on. It would be my entire life. I had to decide, and I didn't know how. I looked at Olivia and saw the pleading look in her eyes. My heart twisted so painfully I wondered if the tart had triggered a major cardiac infarction.

Then I remembered Max's advice for me when I'd been trying to decide on the paint colors. He'd told me to go with my heart. I closed my eyes, and it was a no brainer. "I vote for the dunking booth," I said. "It's always been there, and it should stay."

After the meeting, everyone scattered. I sank back into one of the sofas, feeling utterly defeated. Now that I wanted to keep the inn, I had no feasible way to do that. Grandma's will mandated we sell it.

Olivia paused by the door of the library. "Thanks for all of your help, Wendy."

I smiled at her. "That's what friends are for."

Olivia brushed her red locks over her shoulder, and sighed. "I wasn't much of a friend to you when you first came back."

I looked up at her. "I wasn't much of a friend to you for a bunch of years."

She smiled, leaned down, and hugged me hard. I

finally had my friend back. Lacing my arm through hers, I walked her to the lobby. The others walked out, still exclaiming over how much they loved the inn. Olivia glanced around the lobby. "It will be weird to have different owners here. This is your family's place, and I'll never think of it any other way."

"Me, either." The lump in my throat almost choked me. I grabbed a few little items on the nearest shelf, and rearranged them to keep from having to look at her. She headed for the double doors, stopping with one hand on the knob. "I'll miss you when you leave, Wendy."

"I'll miss you, too. But this time we'll keep in touch. I'll make sure of it," I said, meaning every word.

She walked out, closing the door behind her. I stared at the back of the doors, then turned, and walked back to the windows. I would miss everyone here. I didn't really have anyone in Sacramento, and I had to admit that now. I had friends I loved in Blue Moon Bay. Max was here, too. If he came back like he claimed. Maybe in Tokyo, he'd fall in love with someone else, and stay there just like Ian had. There were no guarantees in life. I'd learned the hard way that people could leave at any given moment.

There was a knock on the door outside the inn. Weird. Maybe it was a new guest, who didn't know we left it open until ten in the evening. I pasted on a polite smile, went to the door, and pulled it open. My smiled died when I recognized the woman on the other side of that door.

"Hello, Wendy, dear. Don't you look wonderful?"

My blood pressure shot dangerously high, and I felt faint. "Mom? What are you doing here?"

****

The inn doors opened further as my mom stepped into the lobby, and I saw Olivia, still outside, staring in at me. She must've seen my mom, because she mouthed "good luck" as the doors closed. Before I could protest, my mom's arms reached out, and wrapped around me.

My stomach plummeted. She had hugged me just like that before. The day she had walked out on me.

"I'm very sorry about your grandma, dear." She pulled back, giving me a better look at her. She had the same dark hair that I had, but her eyes were brown instead of emerald green like my dad's. Her hair was pulled up into a messy knot and she wore a brightly colored skirt, a slim fit tank top, sandals of some kind of woven material with beads running along the top straps, and a wide belt with a giant feather laden buckle.

"I'm surprised to see you." I blinked, shocked that I'd been able to form words. What was she doing here? I took a step back, and nearly tripped over the massive duffel bag sitting there. Mom caught me by one arm, which kept me from falling, but didn't make me feel any better.

I glanced outside where I saw Brian and Max on the back porch. Lucky raced across the deck chasing her Frisbee, and I so wanted to join them.

Mom leaned closer, peering past my shoulder into the inn. She leaned back and looked out toward the grounds before saying, "You really are doing a lot of work here. Grandma would be proud to see you taking it over."

"We're selling it. Remember?" The words stuck in my throat. I felt sick to my stomach. I moved away from the door. "The inn needed a lot of work, and it still needs the work done, but we found buyers who are going to submit an offer, anyway."

Mom poked a finger into her hair, scratched lightly at her scalp. "You must be dreadfully sad to be selling, Wendy. You loved this place."

"How would you know?" The words came out before I could stop them. My face heated but I kept my gaze level.

"Ah, I see." Mom shifted her feet. "You know that eventually you are going to have to discuss this with me, Wendy. It's not going to go away."

"Why are you even here?" I asked, squeezing my fists tight.

She looked over her shoulder at the others gathered on the lawn. "I wanted to pay my respects and see my children. Your father and I had a lovely memorial ceremony for Grandma in Hawaii. We held the ceremony in a garden filled with gorgeous, colorful flowers and a lovely courtyard fountain. I remember the sound of the water, the smell of the flowers, and the beautiful night sky. We lit lanterns then sent them heavenward with their brave little flames . . . it was wonderful."

"She didn't want a ceremony." My eyes burned with tears I could not, and would not shed. My heart ached. I wanted to run outside and collapse into the safety of Max's arms.

Mom tapped her fingers against her hips. "I'm very happy to see you, Wendy. We need to work through our problems, so one day you're happy to see me too."

"I'm not happy to see you." I shook my head, holding back the tears that threatened to come. "You managed to stay gone all this time, why couldn't you stay gone until I'd left?"

Mom's face fell. "We never meant to hurt you."

"Well you did." I flexed my fingers trying to hold everything back, but it had been so many years that I couldn't keep it in any longer. "How did you ever imagine that walking away from your kids was a great parenting move? If you didn't want us you should never have had us. All you ever thought about was yourselves, and when Brian and I got in the way, you just deserted us."

"That isn't how it was, Wendy." She stepped toward me, putting a hand on my arm.

I shook her off, my chest exploding with raw pain. "I remember it very clearly. You and Dad promised we could stay at the inn and finally settle down. Then you both wanted to be free, so you dumped us off like old garbage. You were selfish then, and you're still selfish. If you weren't so selfish you wouldn't be here right now!"

I stormed past her, tears burning my eyes, as I ran out the back door. Max and Brian stared at me with concerned looks, but I flew past them down the steps, heading for the ocean. I jumped off the last step, watching the waves crash into the shore with a low and loud rumble. I made it to the water's edge and stood there, my arms wrapped around my middle and sobs choking me.

"Why did you have to leave me?" I begged, and my words echoed into the air, then vanished in the roar of the surf. But I wasn't talking to my parents. I was calling for the woman I wanted, the one who had always been there for me. I wanted my grandma.

I sobbed harder. She had always been adamant that I had a mom, and that she was my grandma. But in many ways, she had been my mom, too. My grandma had been there for almost all of the firsts in my life: first kiss, first crush, and my first heartache. Grandma had been there for all the little trivial things that made up a teenager's life. Her homemade acne cream had cleared up my skin, her brusque tending had healed up my scraped knees, my bruised heart and my anxiety over starting high school.

My grandma had been there.

My mom hadn't.

But I had walked away from my grandma, just like my parents had walked away from me. I hadn't even considered that she might miss me, and mourn my absence the same way that I mourned theirs. I'd wanted to leave, so I'd left.

"I'm sorry for being selfish, Grandma. I miss you so much," I managed to say through my hiccupping sobs. Everything had gotten so hard. I had fallen back in love with Blue Moon Bay, and with Max, too. I'd fallen in love with having friends I could trust, and who truly knew me.

I'd almost forgotten everything I loved about Sacramento, and that scared me since I was going back. How could I not be excited to put an offer in on my dream house? I wasn't though, and I knew it. How could I even think of giving up everything I'd worked so hard for?

Blue Moon Bay meant more to me. Max meant so much to me. Brian and the inn, Olivia, Megan and the old Pumpkin Festival—even that dunking booth meant so much to me that it hurt to think about leaving it all behind. But when that offer came in I'd have to leave. My chest ached, and I heard a noise. I glanced up to see Max coming down the steps, calling my name.

Chapter Thirteen

I stood on the beach, wiping my eyes as Max came toward me, his sweet dog trotting beside him. He didn't say a word when he reached me, just enveloped me with his arms. I buried my face in the nook of his neck, feeling the heat of his body, and inhaling the irresistible smell of him. His hands rested on my back, his fingers splayed so that they pressed against my spine, and I wondered what it would be like to have him every day for the rest of my life.

"Are you okay?" he asked.

I shook my head. "I don't know."

He released me slowly, then took my hand, and led me for a walk along the beach. The water curled near our feet, and Lucky dashed into the water and out again, yipping happily. She raced over and gave me wet kisses, which made me feel slightly better.

I kicked a large shell back into the water. "My mother's here. I just can't believe she'd come back into town after all of these years, with all I'm dealing with right now."

His brows drew together. "Aren't you happy to see her?"

"Not at all. I don't want to see either of them."

He tightened his arm around me. "Really? I thought you would need them right now. Don't you miss them?"

My chest ached. "I quit missing them a long time ago."

He stopped walking, dropped down onto the sand, and pulled me down next to him. We stared out at the ocean, then he moved his mouth close to my ear. "Don't you want to mend fences with them?"

"No." I squeezed the dry sand between my fingers, then sifted it out slowly.

His forehead creased. "But they're your parents."

"They left me. They walked away and didn't look back."

"They never came back? Ever? She's here now . . ."

Now I was angry with him, too. "So if we had kids and your travel bug coaxed you to leave, then you'd drop the kids off with your mother and call yourself a good parent?" I asked, then squeezed my eyes shut. Now I was discussing his views on parenting our hypothetical children? I was seriously losing it.

His face came closer to mine. I wanted to kiss him. I would've kissed him, too, if I wasn't so angry and confused right now. I reminded myself that Max was not used to staying in one place either, and that he was leaving soon. Just like they had.

"I'm not saying what they did was right, sweetheart." He trailed his finger across my cheek, then held my chin. "They left you. Something I'd never do to you, or to our kids if we had them. There's no denying they messed up. What I don't understand is why you won't forgive them."

My chest cracked, and I blew out a long breath. "Whose side are you on anyway?"

"Yours, Wendy. Always. I think you need to forgive them, though. It will eat you up otherwise, whether you see it or not."

"I don't know if I can ever forgive them." Everything tensed inside me, and I wanted to push thoughts of them aside like I always did. But having them this close made that impossible. I picked up a rock, and threw it into the ocean. "I don't know how they're even here. My mom told me they couldn't afford the airfare. I don't understand how they paid for their flights."

Max's hand tightened around my shoulder, and he glanced away. Then he turned back to me, wearing a pained look. "There's something I need to tell you."

My brows rose. "What?"

He sucked in a breath. "I thought I was doing you a favor. You have to understand that. After the night we met, I overheard you on the phone with your mom. You sounded sad that she couldn't afford the flight out." He raked a hand through his hair. "So I talked to Brian and got their number. To make a long story short, I paid for their airline tickets."

My blood ran cold. "You *paid* for their tickets? You're the reason they're here?"

I didn't wait for any answer to my question, though. I just shot to my feet and ran down the beach, further and further, trying to escape that Max had gone behind my back, and made my worst nightmare come true.

****

The next morning, guilt and remorse were like two little baby lobsters running amok in my belly, creating serious chaos there. After agonizing all night long about the fact that Max had brought my parents here, it seemed obvious he'd done it with the best of intentions.

I had to apologize to Max over the way that I had reacted, and I wanted to do it as soon as possible. Having a rift between us felt like sawing off my arm, and I needed to know things were okay with us. If *he* would forgive *me*.

I noticed I'd slept in until the crazy hour of eleven this morning—it's amazing what no sleep and the lull of the waves could do—then I got dressed, hurried down the stairs, and stopped just inside the entry of the lobby. Brian and Max must've started painting early since there was a fresh coat on the walls. That lovely sea-foam blue looked bright and cheerful.

The whole place was lovely, shining, and perfect. The paintings on the walls and the little sprays of dried flowers in their vases drew my eye. The fresh flowers that Max had brought in the day before lent their fragrance to the room, and the knick-knacks that Grandma had collected over the years were arranged neatly. I knew every single one of those items, and seeing them made memories come up, reminding me of my grandma.

Brian stood behind the desk. He wore a freshly starched shirt and slacks, and he wore a big smile on his face. The guests he was greeting were obviously regulars, since Brian was asking about their granddaughters and the man's golf game. He was good with the guests, much better than I had ever been. Even when we were kids, he'd been good with the guests, and he had always gotten way better tips from them, too. I wondered, once again, why she hadn't left the inn to my brother.

The guests headed out of the lobby, and as I walked to the desk, he handed me a coffee. "You might want to reheat that in the microwave."

"I'm too tired." I sipped the lukewarm liquid, and swallowed. "Nice shirt. Did you suddenly learn to operate the iron or get a heavier mattress?"

"Mom ironed it for me. She also cleaned the lobby. She and Dad were wondering—"

"Don't." I held up a hand. "I really don't want to hear it, Brian. Okay? I haven't had enough coffee to hear anything you have to say about them right now."

He held out his cup. "Would you like mine, too?"

I glared at him. "No."

He set his cup back down. "Just trying to help you out, sis."

"I'm going to work in the office for a bit. Can you hold things down here?"

He gave the empty lobby a pointed look. "I sure will try."

I chose to ignore that and headed off. I hadn't seen Max anywhere downstairs, but I wasn't about to ask Brian if he'd seen him. He got involved in my personal business way too much as it was. I entered the office, looking to see whether or not that formal offer from the Totskys had come in yet.

I checked the fax, but there wasn't anything new there. So I rummaged through a few papers, to check on the occupancy rate at the inn. If there wasn't an offer, I might need those numbers to give the Totskys more information. I was looking through the piles of paper when my phone rang. I checked the screen, hoping it was Max.

Nope. It was Janine.

"Hi, Janine," I said, hoping she had good news.

She spoke in a rush, blowing right through my greeting. "I'm so glad you answered the phone. We have another crisis! The clients that were interested in that house you're brokering over on Sycamore are getting cold feet and Elizabeth is not handling them well. They have been in here all week freaking out on me, and you have to come back or call them as soon as possible. I'm on the verge of a nervous breakdown."

She sounded like it, too. I sighed, wondering if I'd ever been that high strung. Uh, yeah, to the tenth degree. I started pacing the floor. It was frustrating that Elizabeth wasn't cutting it, but it wasn't like her, so she must be having a horrible time with the divorce. "Calm down, Janine. Listen, I've trained you to be a good Realtor, and you can handle this."

Her voice rose an octave, as she said, "I haven't passed my tests yet!"

"I know," I said, trying to sooth her. "That's okay, because you aren't selling them a house. You're helping them make up their minds about a house they already want to buy. Elizabeth can do the paperwork. You just have to do the people work, and you're good at that. Trust me, I know."

"I can't believe you're not having convulsions over this. I thought you'd be on your way back before I even finished the first sentence," she said. "This is a huge commission that we are talking about here. Besides, you always say a crisis with a client deserves our full and undivided attention."

I had said that. But I also used to get up at six in the morning, religiously. I went to the windows and looked out over the green grass to the water that lay beyond. "The clients will get full and undivided attention. Yours. You can do this, and if you learn how to deal with this kind of thing now it will be easier for you in the future."

"Do you mean this kind of thing happens a lot? Maybe I should just keep my assistant position."

I turned away from the windows, tripping over a pile of books someone had set on the floor. I bent over, then picked them up and stacked them on a shelf. "You're going to be fine. Just relax and talk them through it. Point out everything they love about the house. If you keep them away from Elizabeth until the signing, then everything will be fine."

"Okay." She gave a long suffering sigh. "By the way, I heard there's an offer coming in on the townhouse you want to buy. If you're going to make a move, you need to do it fast."

"Thank you, Janine."

"No, thank you. I feel much better now."

I hung up the phone, feeling depressed that someone was bidding on my townhouse. I loved that home. It was gorgeous, and had upgrades like crazy. I had to accept an offer on the inn, before I could submit a contingency offer, though. Maybe it would be a good idea to call the Totskys and ask if they had sent the offer yet. No, that might be too eager. Maybe their offer had come in while I was on the phone?

I went to the fax machine, and, sure enough, there was their offer. Full price, and all cash. I pulled out the papers, and read them. Mrs. Totsky's cover letter wasn't addressed to me, which was odd, but she happily stated they were almost finished finalizing things with the inn. My mouth dropped open as I read the last sentence, then I flipped the page.

The photo in front of me was horrid. It was a hotel that looked like thousands of others, with nothing charming or special about it at all. I flipped back to the previous page and read the final line again, wondering if I'd read it wrong. But I hadn't. The Totskys planned to tear down the Inn at Blue Moon Bay and put up a franchised hotel in its place.

Chapter Fourteen

I walked into Scotty's Seafood Restaurant and the familiar scent of fresh seafood and slow roasting onions, tomatoes and garlic greeted me like an old friend. It was probably a good thing I hadn't eaten much all day because Scotty's was known to be heavy on butter and cream. So heavy that the mayor of Blue Moon Bay had once had a major heart attack while sitting at the table enjoying a hearty special that featured crab and lobster, boiled up with potatoes, corn and whole Vidalia onions, all soaked in drawn sweet butter and seasoned with a large dose of salt.

A petite woman with dark eyes approached, and I smiled at her. She'd been working there for as long as I could remember. "I'm meeting someone, and oh . . . there he is." I pointed to a small booth where Max sat, waving one hand at me. I headed for the table.

Max stood and I went into his arms and hugged him tightly, smelling salt water and cologne on his shirt. My heart beat a little faster as he hugged me back. I'd been worried he'd be upset with me for the way I'd behaved on the beach. He'd vanished all morning, and I'd spent most of the day texting him, but not getting an answer. Part of me wondered if he'd given up on me, and headed off to Tokyo.

When I finally got a text back from him saying he would meet me here for dinner, I was so relieved that I had spun around my room like a giddy teenager. Maybe that's one of the reasons I decided not to delay getting this off my chest. "I'm sorry for getting upset with you yesterday on the beach. And for texting you so much. I don't usually do that, I swear."

He chuckled. "I'm not upset with you, beautiful. I completely understand why you were upset. I'd tried to do a nice thing, but obviously should've checked with you first. I'm sorry."

"You have nothing to be sorry for. But, thanks." I blew out a breath, relieved that he wasn't mad, and it still appeared he wanted to date me. "Should we sit down?"

He released me, and we sat on opposite sides of the table. Max folded his hands on the table top, and I looked down at the carved in names, hearts, and stars that had been there for years.

"Look, that signature is mine, and that's Megan's," I said, smiling.

Max looked down at the table, then wiggled his brows at me. "We'll have to fit our names in here when the waiter's not looking."

"Great idea," I said, laughing. He looked great, too. His hair was a little messy, and his tan was deepening every single day. When he smiled, the tiny lines around his eyes deepened. He just got better looking every time I saw him. I'd never met anyone who could make little butterflies wing around in my belly like he could. Sitting here with Max, everything felt right in my world again. "How do you like Scotty's? Have you been here before?"

He shook his head. "No, this is my first time. I love the décor in here."

I gazed around the place. It hadn't changed at all. The same old woven rope nets hung from the ceilings, the occasional colorful glass ball gleamed from the nets, while everything from old, framed pictures of Blue Moon Bay to school sport uniforms covered the walls. It was wonderfully tacky and funky, and I'd never known until that second how much I adored it.

The view from outside our window was spectacular, all long sweeps of ocean and the marina. The boats lined up in rows, bobbing up and down in the water. I remembered going out on that marina with Max, the night I admitted to myself that I'd fallen for him. It seemed like eons ago, and it was hard to believe I'd ever tried to fight my feelings.

I didn't want to seem like a stage three clinger, but I wondered what he'd been doing all day, and as he sat there silently perusing his menu, my curiosity won out. "So . . . what did you do today?" I asked.

He waited until the server brought us our drinks, took our orders, and left again. Then he gazed across the table with a mischievous look and answered me. "I leased a house in Blue Moon Bay."

My mouth fell open. "What? Why? I thought you were going to Tokyo."

"I'm still going to Japan, for business. But when I come back, this is where I plan to be."

"But you haven't been here very long. You can't be serious."

"I'm entirely serious." He reached across the table and took my hand. His eyes glowed, and the smile on his face was both huge and happy. "I told you Blue Moon Bay was my home, and I meant it. I love the town, the people, and that view." His hand swept toward the windows, and I looked out again at the vast, shining ocean and the sky hovering above it.

"How do you know it's your home?" I asked, truly curious.

"Where to start?" He rubbed his thumb against the back of my hand, sending skittering tingles up my arm. "I love that there is still a Pumpkin Festival, and that people care enough about each other to say hello, and ask how they are doing. I love the crazy patchwork streets and the little downtown area with its cobblestone streets. I love waking up to the sound of surf, and the smell of salty water. I love the Kissed by the Bay legend, and the way people believe it. I love the moon when it's high and full over the ocean. I love everything about this place."

"I love all those things, too. This isn't where my home is, though."

Before he could answer me the server brought our

food. The plates were piled high with fresh shrimp and fish, coleslaw so creamy it begged to be eaten, and plenty of delicious steamed vegetables covered in melted butter. I dug in, not even caring that I might have to loosen a seam on my dress later. Maybe two seams.

The delicious food and Max's company took my mind off my problems, momentarily. But as our meal wound down, I couldn't ignore them anymore. "I received a fax from the couple who want to buy the inn. They intend to tear it down."

Max stopped chewing, then swallowed his bite. "You're going to sell the inn to them?"

"Yes, but we're lucky for that offer since the inn was never officially on the market. It isn't even show-ready. Tearing down the inn will be devastating, and Brian's going to hate me."

"He loves you, beautiful. You have to know that," he said, then his expression changed. He raked his fingers through his thick, dark hair. "I'm stunned that you're accepting the offer, especially knowing the buyers will tear it down. You love the inn, Wendy. I thought you'd change your mind, and keep it. Don't you think your grandma thought that, too?"

My eyes blurred. I had no idea what my grandma had been thinking. "I c-can't keep the inn. I'm going back to Sacramento."

A line formed between his brows. "I'm thrown by this. I never thought you'd sell. . . But, no matter what happens with the inn, I'm not going anywhere. If you're in Sacramento, we'll still see each other. We'll figure something out."

He was always trying to make this work. I wanted us to work, too, but it was impossible. Deep down, he had to know that. "Max, long distance relationships never work out."

"Why not?"

"You travel for long periods of time. Plus, I am a Realtor so I work crazy hours. Put that together, and we'll never see each other. We'll drift apart and—"

"Have some faith in me, beautiful. In *us*. I'm sure we could work that out with a little scheduling. Plus, for someone who doesn't like traveling, you've shared a lot of happy memories of doing just that."

A small laugh escaped. "You're right on that point. I

did like traveling with my parents. Just not *all* the time." I squeezed the napkin in my lap, afraid things wouldn't work out with us, and also afraid to hope that they *could* work out. Both were equally scary. "Our lives are so different, Max. We're so different."

He merely grinned at me. "I think we're a lot alike. We're both ambitious and determined to succeed on our own terms. We would make an amazing team."

"People get lonely when they're in a long distance relationship," I said, softly.

"I imagine those people get lonelier when they are in no relationship at all," he countered.

"You have an answer for everything." I smiled, loving his optimism. Finally, I threw my hands up. "Are you going to eat the rest of that?"

He looked down at the particularly tasty looking large shrimp on his plate, stabbed it with his fork, and lifted it to my mouth. "It's all yours, beautiful."

I took the bite, savoring the delicious favor, and savoring my evening here with Max. A bar of sunlight came through the window, illuminating his face and it hit me again, that I-can't-even-breathe feeling ensued. Ah, heaven.

"Now that we've finished dinner. Are you up for dessert?" he asked.

I patted my bulging belly, and shook my head. "If I ate another bite, I'd have to walk around in yoga pants for the next week," I said, then giggled.

He suggested a walk on the beach instead. That was the best offer I'd had all day. Maybe it would take my mind off the fact that I had to sell my beloved family inn to those vultures, and that soon the only home I'd ever known would be gone.

****

I walked into Bay Side Coffee the next morning, and the barista smiled, lifting a hand in greeting. I waved back. There were plenty of tables open, and I spotted Megan and Olivia already waiting at one of them. I stopped, surprised. I hadn't known Olivia would be here and I wondered if someone else was joining us, since there were already three cups on the table. This was supposed to be a business meeting. Had Megan turned it into a girls get together?

I didn't mind if she had. Seeing them together made a

lump rise in my throat. When we had been teenagers, we had met at Blue Moon Burgers almost every day. I missed that ritual, and I'd miss them when I went back to Sacramento.

That halted my feet. These were my friends, but would they still be my friends after I sold the inn to developers? Neither of them wanted to see it torn down, but it wasn't like I had a choice. I hoped Brian, and everyone understood there was nothing else I could do.

Olivia caught my eye and waved. "This coffee isn't going to stay hot forever, you know."

I headed for their table, then dropped in the chair, reaching for the cup Olivia pushed toward me.

Megan raised her brows. "Do you want to share this chocolate scone with me? I asked Olivia already, and she practically forked the sign of the evil eye at me."

Olivia sighed. "Those things should be illegal. They are just pastry covered death you know."

"I'll take a little pastry covered death," I said. "We can't have you dying alone."

Megan cut the scone in half with a little plastic knife, and I took a section, biting into it while Olivia made a face.

Olivia sipped her coffee. "How are you? You look better than I thought you would after seeing your mom the other day."

I swallowed the bite of pastry, and rich chocolate. "Yeah, it's been hard having her at the inn. She and my dad are holding Grandma's memorial today. Brian and I are supposed to attend."

Olivia gave me an odd look. "Oh, I thought your grandma didn't want a memorial service."

"She didn't. But my parents decided they wanted to have one for her anyway."

Megan chewed thoughtfully. "Well, it must be nice to see your parents again. I know you must miss them."

I bristled. "They're driving me crazy."

"Come on, Wendy." Megan shot me a look that said I wasn't fooling her. "You may be mad at your parents, but we know you love them. Besides, your parents are cool in a hippy fly-by-night kind of way. I'm sure the memorial is at least going to be interesting."

I leaned back in my chair. "That is definitely one way to put it."

Olivia sighed. "Wendy, I know what they did hurt you. But you need to let that go, and forgive them."

I took a long sip of my coffee. "Everyone keeps saying that to me, but I don't know how."

"You just do it," Olivia said, fingering the lip on her coffee cup. " Remember how I told you my parents separated? Well, I didn't tell you they broke up because my mom reconnected with an old high school flame online. She left my dad for him."

My mouth fell open. When we were young, Olivia's parents had been so happy. Plus, her mom was so nice. I would never have imagined she could do something like that. "But your mom loves your dad. It was so obvious."

Her gaze drifted downward, and she studied the table. "Yes, she did love him. She loves us. But she left anyway. The worst part is that I'm the one who got her onto the social media site, where they reconnected. In a way, I was the catalyst, which sucks. She hurt me, and believe me I'm mad. I still love her, though. I'm going to forgive her, too. I don't understand why she's acting this way, but she must have her own reasons."

Like my parents had their reasons for leaving us with

Grandma. Could forgiving them be that simple? I reached out, and touched her arm lightly. She looked down at my hand, smiled, then covered it with her own. "I'll try my best. That's all I can promise," I said.

She smiled back at me. "Fair enough."

I changed the subject by asking, "Have you gone back out on the boat with Mr. Perfect lately?"

"Yes, and believe it or not, I get less nervous each time." She smiled, and turned to Megan. "You going to start dating again?"

Megan made a face, as she dipped her finger into the pastry crumbs. "The way I feel right now, I might join a single-for-life program. At least I have my work. Speaking of which, I have your website finished. Do you want to see it?"

"Absolutely." I wanted to tell her to never mind, since the new owners were just going to tear my beloved inn down, but I couldn't give her the bad news since she was obviously so proud of her work.

Megan dug around in her bag and pulled out her laptop then booted it up. She hit a few keys then pushed it over to me. I stared at the screen. The ocean spread out, glittering and shimmering under a large blue moon hanging slightly low over the water. A whale appeared, leaping high into the sky, its back brushing against the bottom curve of the moon. The whale splashed back into the ocean and the water formed the words, "Blue Moon Bay, Live the Legend." The words vanished and a couple appeared embracing on the beach.

Megan beamed and peeked around the corner of the laptop while Olivia leaned in close to watch the whole scene play out again. Megan asked, "Isn't that awesome?"

It was awesome, like a sweet romantic movie, where you could also book a room at an inn. What it was not, was the straightforward, business-like website that I had envisioned. It was fanciful and cutesy, and I loved it. I hated to break the news to her that the inn was going to be torn down. A little voice in my head urged me to tell her the truth, but I couldn't when she looked so happy. "Launch it," I said.

Chapter Fifteen

We all gathered near the end of the spit, the same spot where the Blue Moon Bay lovers had said goodbye to each other and sworn their vows by the light of the blue moon. It was a perfect afternoon, the sky hung above us, a long lovely expanse of solid blue, not a single cloud in sight. The ocean stretched beyond us, its rim meeting the horizon, and the two things met and blended there, giving the impression of utter infinity.

Mom and Dad had set out huge sky lanterns for each of us to light later. The crisp white domes of the lanterns poked up from the green grass, making a stunning contrast that I could not stop looking at. They had brought out a low table filled with cake, wine, and flowers. Long streamers of red and yellow fabric that rippled in the low breeze swaddled every available surface and Mom stood near the table, lighting dozens of fragrant candles while Dad began to beat a small drum slowly. The sound of that drum was low, deep, and mournful.

Brian stood next to me, tilting his head toward mine. "Well, it is colorful, isn't it?"

I shot him a "whatever" look. Mom and Dad had insisted that we all wear yellow and red, too, and I was far from happy about it. "We look like escapees from some time-travelling disco. Grandma would die again if she saw us like this. You know we should be wearing black, and she would have been the first to say so."

Brian glanced down at his yellow shirt. He had tucked a piece of red fabric in the pocket and Mom had made him a little belt thing out of twisted together yellow and red fabric. "It is a bit bright. I guess it's a good thing we weren't drinking last night."

"Speak for yourself," I muttered.

Brian chuckled. "I was speaking for you. I was definitely drinking last night. I had no idea that you were, too. On the plus side, I think I can wear this get up to the Pumpkin Festival."

I gave the outfit a glance. "Will you be working as a clown?"

Brian waved the colorful flowers he held, almost hitting me in the nose with them. I managed, barely, to suppress the urge to wave my own bouquet right in his face. "That's not nice, Wendy. But for your information, I am going to be a clown. Megan talked me into it. She said Olivia was sad that the old tradition was going by the wayside."

"Clowns are freaky," I whispered. I'd definitely be snapping pictures of him in the outfit and using it for blackmail with his kids someday.

Mom began to hum along with the drum. It was oddly soothing and pretty but I wished they would stop already and finish up the memorial they had insisted upon. Mom started walking around in a circle.

I leaned toward my brother, since he was the only other sane person here. "What is she doing?" I asked.

Brian answered in a cheerful voice. "No idea. Just go with it."

"I saw Olivia and Megan this morning."

"Megan?" He fiddled with the makeshift belt. "What's new with her?"

"She's getting over that guy from the yacht club. But that's not why I told you about running into them. It's Olivia. She told me her mom cheated on her dad, and moved out. You know what else she said?"

"No, are you going to tell me?"

"She said she's going to forgive her mom for doing it."

Brian nodded. "Good for her."

"She said I should forgive Mom and Dad."

Brian grinned. "You should. It's about time."

I stared at my mom, who was now doing some comical dance near the waves. "I don't know how. She abandoned us."

"We survived. Just forgive them, Wendy. It takes less effort than holding a grudge."

I took a long breath. "Is that what you did? You just forgave them?"

"Yes."

"How? I mean don't you remember what they did?"

He frowned. "Of course I do. But they're my parents and I love them. I don't have to understand them to love them, you know. Besides, it wasn't like they just dumped us off in an orphanage or something. They tried to stay here and make it work. They just couldn't. It's dumb to keep being mad over something that happened a long time ago."

I remembered them trying to make it work, for four whole months. Maybe that had been hard for them, though. Who knew? I wanted to forgive them, but it was hard. I closed my eyes. "I'm going to work on forgiving them."

His hand came up, and squeezed my shoulder. "Good. That would be good."

It would be good. I had carried around that anger for far too long, and it had been a heavy burden. I made up my mind right then that forgiving them was exactly what I was going to do.

Mom stopped dancing, and turned to us. "I want to share a memory of your grandma with you. The very first time I met her, she was out here on this very sand. She was wearing a bright blue dress and she was walking on the beach. She was the first and only person I'd ever seen walking the beach in dress shoes. Her hair was perfect, not a strand out of place.

"I was so nervous I could barely talk. Your dad had just asked me to marry him, and he brought me here to meet her that same night. It was scary, and as soon as I saw her I just knew she was going to tell him that there was no way she would give us her blessing.

"She was so proper and neat, and there I was in a halter dress, holding my shoes in one hand and with my hair all messy from the wind. Your dad walked right up to her and said, 'Mom, this is the woman I am going to marry,' and she came over to me, and hugged me. She smelled like that perfume she always wore, lavender and seawater, and she said, 'He's a good man, and one you can count on.' She was right, too. He is a good man, and I have always been able to count on him."

Brian plucked at his bouquet, sending petals down onto the grass. I grabbed his hand, and gave him a look. He stared at me, and stopped immediately. I whispered, "You know what else I remember? That she promised to come here for my sixteenth birthday. She didn't, and that is hard to forgive. I waited up all night." I pointed at the inn behind us. "I sat right there by the windows, waiting for her to come up the driveway, and she never did."

Brian shushed me, and turned back toward Mom, who was still talking. "When we got married she made our wedding cake, because she didn't trust anyone in town to do it."

I edged toward my brother. "Or, what about the times they were supposed to come back for our graduations? They didn't make those either. That's pretty unforgivable."

Brian elbowed me this time. "Chill out."

I glared at him. "Or, how about that time when she promised to—"

"If you're going to forgive them, then you have to forgive all of it. Now *hush*."

Dad shot us a weird look, and we straightened, then stared forward.

Mom brought her hands together in the prayer position. "Oh, she was so romantic."

"Romantic?" The word burst out of my mouth before I could stop it. "Are you talking about Grandma? She was not at all romantic."

"Why yes, she was," she said, sounding flustered.

I shook my head, adamantly. "Grandma wasn't like that at all. She was the most unromantic person alive, and you'd know that if you'd stuck around."

Brian hissed at me. "What happened to forgiveness?"

he asked.

"That ship sailed when Mom said Grandma was romantic. Please. She's the woman who told me that if I really thought I was in love with Ian McBride then I was either terminally ill or out of my mind. Turned out she was right. The second one."

"Ian McBride was a poser," Brian said mildly. "Everyone knew it, but you."

My face reddened. "Take that back. I hadn't developed good taste in guys yet. He was my first love, though, and if Grandma had been romantic she would have understood that."

Mom raised her hands in the air, then lowered them slowly. "Wendy, please. We knew her well before you did. Plus, we were grownups when we knew her, so our perceptions are different than yours."

I crossed my arms. "You mean she didn't have to raise you."

Instead of taking offense, she took on a thoughtful look. "Well, she sort of did. I was lacking in a lot of ways. Do you know I had never cooked a meal before I moved into the inn?"

I blinked. "No, I didn't know that."

Mom looked pleased. "It's true. She taught me to cook. I remember the first time I tried to fry chicken. It came out burned on the outside and raw in the middle. It was awful."

"You never fed us burned chicken." I had to give her that. Mom was always a good cook.

"That's because she taught me how to cook it properly. She always said that my chicken that first night was the most charred chicken she'd ever seen. She was the one person I never wanted to disappoint."

I stepped forward. "But Grandma didn't even want a memorial, and you're ignoring her wishes. Don't you think that would disappoint her?"

She shook her head. "Memorials aren't for the ones who leave us. They're for those who get left behind."

"Well, you left us behind," I retorted. "Should we have had a memorial for the two of you?"

Mom sputtered. "That is hardly the same. You can't still be holding onto all of that, can you? It's silly to hold onto anger over things that happened so long ago. Brian isn't holding on to any bad feelings. Isn't that right? Tell her, Brian."

He glanced away, then inhaled deeply. "I think her emotions are valid, Mom."

My emotions were valid? Really? Mom's mouth curved downward, and I gaped at Brian like he was nuts. I was pretty sure he was, or that his brain had been hijacked by the alien horde.

I raised a brow. "Emotionally valid?"

"I got it from reality TV." His cheeks turned pink, and his eyes were glassy. Uh, oh. He was close to tears. My heart twisted in my chest. He had stood up for me, but he'd only done it out of loyalty. It's not like he'd been sincere. He'd already told me he thought it was stupid to keep being mad at them, and it meant a lot to me that he'd taken my side anyway.

Dad lit the lanterns, making it clear he was doing his best to save this memorial, or at least turn it around. The lanterns floated upward, and tears came to my eyes. I'd sincerely wanted to forgive them for leaving, but all I could think about was the times I'd needed them, and they hadn't been there for me. Like Olivia had said, they must have had their reasons, or whatever, but I couldn't get past the facts.

But why did their reasons make what they did any better? How did they have the right to get what they needed—to travel, and live their nomadic life—when I didn't have a choice in where I lived? Why did I have to forgive them for my needing parents? I was the younger person, so why should I have to be the bigger one?

Mom wandered to the edge of the water and Dad went to her. The sound of her sobs floated toward me. Brian walked in their direction a few steps, leaving me standing there alone.

Mom broke out of Dad's arms, spinning to face me, and cried, "Fine, Wendy. I will stay here forever if that's what it takes to have a relationship with you. All I've *ever* wanted was a relationship with you! We'll find a place in Blue Moon Bay and settle down. Will that fix things?"

My mouth dropped open, but no words came out. This was the moment I'd been waiting for my entire life—to have my family together and stable and happy. But something didn't feel quite right. In the corner of my mind, I pictured my grandma's face and that harsh line between her brows when she wasn't pleased. Unfortunately, I had no idea what she was trying to tell me.

****

The next morning, Brian and I were shocked to receive another offer on the inn, from a company that beat the Totskys's price. After a long discussion, we accepted the second offer instead. It broke my heart to sell the inn, but the will required us to accept the offer, since it was well above market price, and at least this way there was a chance the new owners would keep the inn running, and not tear it down. Brian was melancholy and I tried not to think about losing the inn, because there was nothing we could do about it now. It was done.

The new cappuccino machine arrived, and was a tiny bright spot in my morning. With the heavy sadness inside me, I grasped for whatever happiness I could find, before we had to leave the inn for good. I set the espresso machine on its own table in the lobby so that guests could use it, too. But right then, Max and I were the only ones near the blessed machine. We were discussing the pros and cons of espresso versus drip, while waiting for the hot water to spew through the fresh grounds I'd tamped down moments ago.

"I'll miss the gang at Bay Side Coffee, but I need my first cup as soon as possible in the mornings," I told him, trying to keep my mind off the elephant in the room. I hadn't told Max about the new offer, because then it would feel more real.

"Getting caffeine in your system is a big requirement for you, huh? I'll have to remember that." Max laughed, the sound warming my heart. I hugged him impulsively, and caught a whiff of his enticing aftershave above the delectable smell of the cappuccino. Everything would work out the way it was supposed to. I had to believe that.

Behind us, one of the arriving guests stood at the front desk talking to Brian. He was a regular, and excited about the renovations. Right now he was raving about our new website and brochures, calling them genius and creative. Way to go, Megan!

"I've never seen anything so interesting and wonderful." The man's voice carried slightly, as Max poured the espresso shots into my cup. "Can you tell me the name of your web designer? My boss wants to revamp her site, and I'd love to recommend the person you used."

Brian gave him Megan's business card, and sang her praises.

I smiled at Max, but it was bittersweet. In many ways, I felt happier than I had in a long time—maybe ever. But the good things in my life were tinged with a dark cloud, because we were losing the inn, my biggest memory of my grandma. With that sad thought, I poured milk and sugar into my cup, and stirred.

The lobby doors opened. My gaze darted that way, expecting to see a guest coming in, but instead it was *them* . . . the Totskys, who had lied to us about running the inn, just so they could buy the property for its oceanfront views. I pasted a smile on my face, determined to be professional, and headed toward them.

Mrs. Totsky strode across the lobby in her high heels, with Mr. Totsky close behind her. "Ms. Watts, I'm pleased to see you. I've left you messages, but haven't heard back from you."

I gripped my coffee cup in one hand and forced my

brightest smile, which was physically painful. "Yes, I received your messages, and your offer."

"Well, that's good to know." Her smile looked just as forced as mine, and I wondered if she was gritting her teeth like I was. "We decided to drop by your darling inn, because we hadn't heard back from you on the offer, which, as you'll recall, was full price."

"Thank you, but we're not accepting it," I said, without the slightest hint of emotion in my voice. With my gaze on hers, I took a long slow sip of my drink.

Tiny lines appeared on either side of her mouth. "Is there another offer? If that's the case, we're certainly willing to surpass it. We just love this beautiful inn. It has a special place in our hearts."

My stomach clenched, and my smile wavered. "Right."

She looked nonplussed. "I'm sorry?"

"Me, too." I knew she wasn't saying what I pretended to have heard, but it was worth a shot. Maybe they would just walk away now, and spare us all a scene. I knew that I shouldn't mix business with my personal feelings, but in the case of my grandma's inn, the two were forever intertwined, and my patience had quickly deteriorated.

"I think perhaps you should reconsider." Mrs. Totsky's voice took on a shrill tone, and her smile mirrored a shark's grin. So much for them walking away without making a scene. "We can go a lot higher, and we will. We truly want this inn. Name your price."

"I'm not willing to reconsider, Mrs. Totsky." I tipped the cappuccino to my lips, and stole a peek at Max. He leaned against the wall, and crossed one foot over the other, a proud smile on his full lips.

Mrs. Totsky's face paled. "This is ludicrous. We agreed to your price, so we have a contract."

"I'm sorry you think so, but I didn't accept your offer. I have the right to field offers, and to reject them as I see fit. I've seen fit to reject yours. Neither of you will be able to purchase this inn, not for any amount of money and that is my final say."

Her cheeks turned pink, and her brightly painted lips pursed. "You're being incredibly obstinate!"

I narrowed my eyes at her. "That's better than being unscrupulous. We know your true plans were to tear the inn down, and build a new hotel here."

Everyone was quiet. The old timer stood at the front desk, his head wobbling back and forth like he was watching a tennis match. Brian leaned across the podium, and Max stood where he had been, that smile growing wider with every single second.

Mrs. Totsky choked out, "That is not *true*."

"Unfortunately, it is." I advanced toward them, and she took a step back. "I saw your hotel plans, since you attached them to your offer. Let me know if this rings any bells. Your intentions were to build a concrete monstrosity, with too many windows on one side and not enough on the other. The place had no charm, no quirks, and no heart. I won't allow you to do such a thing on my ancestral property. Period."

Mrs. Totsky turned to her husband, whose face had gone white. "What did you do? You sent her the plans? Have you lost your mind?" she barked, then turned to me, her expression reeking of desperation. She held her hands out in a pleading gesture. "We can't lose this deal. There must be some price you'll take."

I shook my head. "Your offer was rejected. Accept it, Mrs. Totsky. There is absolutely nothing you can do or say that would make me change my mind. In fact, we reserve the right to refuse service to anyone, and I am refusing you right here and now. It's time for you to leave."

Mrs. Totsky huffed, tightened her purse on her shoulder, then stormed out. Her husband trailed on her heels, and I had the feeling he was going to be in deep trouble.

Brian smiled at me from behind the desk. "Nice going, sis."

The man behind the counter fiddled with his room keys. "I'm happy to hear nothing will happen to this inn. If it were up to me, it would be made into a historic landmark."

"That's what I keep saying." I smiled at the man, who nodded before going down the hall with his luggage. Max came up beside me, put his arm around my waist, and I leaned into him.

Laughter floated in from the back porch. Moments later, Mom and Dad came walking through the door. She held a bouquet of flowers she had picked somewhere. She'd also twined some of the colorful blooms into her hair, and Dad was laughing. They were holding hands, still in love after all of these years. They had met right out there on that very same beach where I had met Max. Maybe they'd even kissed under a blue moon.

A lump hit my throat. Everything I cared about was here, and I'd been blind not to see it before. Max was here. Brian was here. My friends, and Mom and Dad were here—and this time they promised to stay. Even the silly old Pumpkin Festival was here. But all of the love originated with Grandma's inn.

We'd gotten rid of the Totskys, but we had no way of knowing what the new owners planned to do with the inn. I closed my eyes, sending thoughts to the universe, begging that my home wouldn't be torn down, and that the inn would live on forever.

Chapter Sixteen

It had been a week since we'd turned down the liars' offer, and accepted the new one. Escrow was moving along as planned, and the buyer's · lawyer was professional, but discreet, despite my incessant inquiries of his client's plans with the inn.

To keep my looming fear that the buyer might be a developer at bay, I tried to keep busy. Max rented a sailboat, and we went out for long sails on smooth waters. His kisses were a warm escape, and we were growing closer every single day.

I'd found my grandma's big hat in her closet, still in the box. I wore it for a walk on the beach, and instead of feeling pain this time, it made me feel as if she were still with me.

Mom and Dad had fallen back in love with Blue Moon Bay, so Brian and I spent a lot of time with them just exploring the town and its surroundings. Mom was good to have around, because she could cook like nobody's business. It felt like we were finally a family—

the family we were supposed to have been this entire time.

I slept in again, as per my new routine, and I even stayed in bed listening to the sound of the waves. Then I walked down to the lobby, and began making a cappuccino. Brian wasn't at the front desk and I frowned, wondering where he was. I finished steaming the milk with the little wand, then headed into the dining room, but nobody was there either.

What was going on? Mom and Dad were usually having their breakfast right now, but the table was completely bare. It didn't look like anyone had been in there at all this morning. Maybe they had gone out for breakfast? Brian was addicted to those pancakes down at the diner, and Mom and Dad liked them, too.

Since I'd slept in again, maybe they had gone on without me. I shook my head and went back into the lobby. That was when I noticed Max wasn't around either, and neither was Lucky. Usually, at this time of day, the two of them were romping along the beach, working out the energy she always had after a good long sleep.

But they weren't out there. Nobody was around. Where was everyone?

I walked to the back porch and peeked out. Several guests sat in the Adirondack chairs, but no Max. Huh. Had he gone to the diner with my family? He spent a lot of time with them, so it was possible. Weird that he hadn't left me a note or a text.

My phone rang, interrupting my thoughts. Maybe it was Max. I glanced at the screen, which illuminated Janine's name. With a frown, I answered her call. "Hi, Janine."

"Wendy, I hate to tell you this, but someone bought your townhouse," she said.

I paused for a second, waiting for the pang of regret. But it never came. The house of my dreams was gone, but it was okay. My dreams had changed and that townhouse was not part of the new plan. I'd be staying in Blue Moon Bay.

"Oh, well, someone is very lucky. It's a great place." I walked to the table and looked down at the guest book, checking to see if anyone had checked in that morning.

"That really should have been your house, but there is

another one that came up down the street that is similar if you're interested. Maybe all is not lost?"

I had to smile. "No, all is not lost."

Janine sounded relieved. "Does that mean you're coming back?"

I ran a finger down the guest book's carefully kept pages. "No, I'm not."

Janine sounded horrified now. "But what about your career? You were such a great Realtor. Your face is on billboards all over the city. You're my idol. What will I do without you?"

"There is more to life than work, Janine. It's important, but it's not my priority anymore." I was planning to give up my business in Sacramento, and move back here to be close to my family, and Max. I hung up, my mind going back to the question of where everyone had disappeared to this morning.

I walked to Max's room and raised my hand to knock, but my hand stalled midair as I heard his voice coming through the phone.

"Dad, I know you're upset that I backed out of the project, but it couldn't be helped. Yes, I'm still going to

Japan as we agreed. I'll head over there in a day or two . . . I know you want me to run the business there . . . I can absolutely set it up and get it running in a matter of months, no problem . . ."

He was leaving for Japan and he'd be gone for months? Maybe even forever, like Ian had—only this time would be worse. I was so much more in love with Max than I'd ever been with anyone before. Tears blinded me as my worst fears came true. Again. This was exactly why I hadn't wanted to get involved with Max. But his dad must've put too much pressure on him. Now, it was settled. For him anyway. I, on the other hand, felt devastated.

****

I turned and ran. The sound of my footsteps along the wooden floors was very loud but I didn't care. I almost ran into the banister, and when I hit the turn in the landing I nearly lost my footing. For one second I had an awful vision of my body tumbling down the stairs and landing hard at the bottom. That would be just my rotten luck.

I heard Max's door open and he called out my name,

but I didn't stop. My heart had shattered into millions of pieces, and every shard sent fresh pain into my entire body.

He was going away just when I'd gotten used to him being here, and just when I thought we really had a shot at that stupid happily ever after thing. I knew he had planned to go to Tokyo temporarily, but not for months. People grew apart in that amount of time, and met other people.

I knew better. I knew that people left. It was what they did, and had always done. I knew that from hard experience. I hit the back porch, stubbed my toe on the top step, and grunted loudly as I flew down the steps and headed to the beach.

My vision blurred and doubled as my feet met the sand. Sand spurted out from under my feet and I stopped just short of the waves, which were raging and hissing today. That was apt and I stood there, staring at the white curds of foam cresting and spitting onto the sand.

"Wendy!" Max's voice came from behind me. I didn't turn around. I considered running right into the waves in a huge tragic gesture, but the water curling over my toes was too cold to really give that a try.

Lucky didn't think the water was too cold. She ran out in front of me and began to romp in the waves joyfully. Max came up beside me and said, "Wendy, talk to me. What's going on?"

"How could you do that to me?" My voice was sharp, but so was the pain in my heart. "How could you do that and not even tell me!"

"How did you find out . . .?" His voice trailed off and he spread his hands wide, palms toward the ground in a calming gesture. "Let me explain, please. Originally, my dad heard the inn might go on the market, and that's why I came here that day. But I canceled that project with my dad after I met you. I told him we couldn't buy the inn, because I could see how special it was to you and your family."

My jaw nearly hit the ground, and my body went numb. What in the world was Max saying to me? He wasn't talking about Japan. It sounded like he'd wanted to buy my inn. That did not compute, not one little bit.

"Last week the offer from the Totskys came in and I had no choice but to submit a higher offer through my company. I couldn't let it go to those sharks, not when they were just going to rip it down. I would've told you the offer you accepted was from me, but I wanted to give you time to change your mind. I've been waiting for you to tell me you regretted accepting the offer, so I could cancel it. But you haven't done that."

I was too confused and hurt to be calm. I sort of wanted to kick the nearest thing, but since the nearest thing was Max I stifled that urge. "You're the one who's buying my inn? You betrayed me? You *lied* to me?"

"Didn't you know?" He gripped both sides of his head, then let his hands fall to his waist. "I didn't tell you I was initially interested in buying the inn, because I thought after you did all that work to fix it up, you would keep it, and run it with Brian like your grandma wanted. At that point, it wouldn't have mattered that I'd planned to buy it, because you wouldn't be selling it anyway. But then the Totskys's offer came in and I had no choice."

My legs went weak and it was amazing I didn't fall over. "Y-You only helped us fix the inn up, because you were buying it yourself. You didn't help because you cared about me. You were only looking at your bottom line, just like your parents trained you to do!" The words came out in a shout, but the hurt exploded from me.

Max shook his head and kicked an incoming wave but it did no good. The water just broke over the toe of his shoe and ran back into the incoming tide. He growled, and ran his hands through his hair. "That is absolutely *not* true. Why can't you trust me, Wendy? I helped you with the inn because I wanted to help you, not because my life would be easier if the place was already renovated before I bought it. I worked on the inn to spend time with you, and because I was hoping you would see the inn for how beautiful it is, and want to stay."

I took a deep breath. Thinking when I'm hurt was not my strong suit. I walked toward the plaque that told the story of the Kissed by the Bay legend and stood there, trying to breathe, trying to think. But all I could concentrate on was how fake that legend was, and how like that pathetic woman I was. Only she had never been betrayed like I had been, and by the very man I'd thought could make the legend come true for me.

The water was loud, roaring in my ears as it screamed and beat against the shore. Max walked up beside me.

"Wendy, you're being unreasonable."

I glared at him. "I'm being unreasonable? I didn't try to buy your company and not tell you!"

"This is a problem that can be solved. I should've told you, but I didn't. I'm sorry. It happened and it's over. Why can't you ever just let things go?"

Let things go? He'd bought my inn behind my back! I turned to him with a stony stare. "I'm good at letting things go, actually."

Hurt showed in his face. It stung my heart, but it was too late to take the words back, and what was more I didn't want to. "Are you talking about letting *me* go?" He turned away, and then he faced me again. "This is ridiculous. If you don't want to sell the inn, if you're so hurt by that, then why don't you just keep it?"

My eyes ached. The wind picked up and the sand and grit blew against my lower legs and feet. I shook my head. "I can't keep it."

"You don't want to," he said, firmly.

I lifted my hands and dropped them again. "No. I can't. My grandma's will won't allow us to keep the inn. We have to sell it."

His mouth fell open. He stepped back, then took a step toward me. I could see his mind reeling. "If you had told me that . . ."

My fists balled at my sides. "I didn't know you well enough to tell you!"

Max straightened. "Is that right? You don't know me well enough to tell me that. You don't trust me enough to tell me, and you don't trust me enough to believe that I helped you because I wanted to, not because of a bottom line. Wow, Wendy. I don't even know what to say to that."

I jabbed my finger toward the ground. "You didn't trust me either. You never told me you had put in that offer."

He blew out a breath. "I didn't think it mattered."

I looked over at the plaque. I wanted to believe him, but how could I believe that? How could I believe that he had just helped me because he wanted to, and not because he wanted the inn? How could I believe any of what he told me, or how I felt about him? How could I even believe that what he felt about me was real? That offer floated between us, a poisoned cloud that made everything between us seem dark and wrong.

"It matters, Max. It matters a whole lot. You should have told me."

He stared me down. "And you should have told me about your grandma's will."

I crossed my arms, shivering in the breeze. "Well, I didn't. I can't change that now."

He leaned closer. I wanted to let him put his arms around me and hold me tightly. I wanted to bury my face in his shirt and smell his cologne and the soap he bathed with. I couldn't do that, though. Pain and doubt wracked through my body, and I had to be strong to protect myself.

He held his palms up. "We both did something that wasn't right. I admit that I should have told you. I wish I had. I didn't mean to put a wedge between us, and after I started helping you and falling for you, I feared what brought me here, what brought me to *you*, might hurt us. So I said nothing. I'm sorry. I'm asking you to forgive me. I'm asking you to trust me. If you can't, or won't, things can never be right between us. You have to know that."

I did know that. I just didn't know how to let go of the pain and the confusion. I didn't know how to believe that he had done everything he had for me, and not for his business.

"Trust you?" My voice was hoarse. "When I just found out you're going to Japan for *months*. You never told me that, either." I kicked a seashell back into the water, watching it sink until it disappeared.

He sighed, staring out at the water. "Wendy, it is just temporary. How long I'll be gone is still in negotiations."

"You'll never settle down. You're too much like my parents." I kicked a few more shells and a couple of pebbles into the water. Little spouts of water shot up, mirroring my emotions.

"Please don't judge me based on your parents. It might be high time you stopped feeling abandoned every time someone has to go away for a little while."

He didn't usually talk to me like that. He sounded a bit angry, and I felt shame at his words. Brian told me I needed to let the pain go, and now Max was basically saying the same thing. They were right. I had spent so much of my life feeling like the orphaned kid, and it was starting to wear thin but that didn't mean I knew how to let go of the pain.

I opened my mouth to say something, but he cupped my face in his hands. "This business is only temporary. I'm coming back. This is home for me. I'm not leaving this town . . . or you. Can't you see that? Can't you believe in me?"

I wanted to believe. But all I could see was everything ending.

A huge splash of water landed on my legs. I turned to see Lucky gamboling about in the waves. Just as I turned my head to look she shook her entire body, sending more water spraying across us. Great, I'd smell like wet dog on top of everything else.

"I just don't see how we can work through this." I dropped my head back, staring at the cloudy sky, hoping for an answer. But I couldn't see one. "I don't know how to let the hurt go . . ."

He kissed me. His mouth came down on mine, warm and firm and I closed my eyes, letting my body sag into his. His arms went around me, and I let him hold me. The bits and pieces of my heart were poking holes through my skin. I could feel myself bleeding from every little prick.

He broke the kiss off, and looked me in the eye. "Relationships are like a roller coaster ride. There are ups and downs, fast turns, and drops. You can't give up when you're hurt. You have to fight for us, Wendy. If you care about me, you will."

My throat went dry. "We can't make it work if you're not here. I can't do long distance, and I've told you that the entire time. Plus, you lied to me. I don't know how to get past that. We can't work this out, and never should've started anything in the first place. I'm sorry."

His eyes flickered with pain and I turned away, heading back up the steps to the inn. Lucky let out a long howl. I wanted to turn around, but I was afraid to look at Max. I'd hurt him, and I'd hurt myself, too. But it was better to hurt now than later, say in a month, when he stopped calling and he didn't come back like he'd planned.

I'd been hurt before, and could still feel the phantom pain. But going through that over Max would be so much worse. I loved him. If he forgot about me, I'd never recover. He said he'd come back, but I couldn't trust his words when he'd been lying to me this entire time. It was better to break it off now and grieve for a little while, than sit around for months, suspended and waiting, for the worse pain that was sure to come.

****

My feet hit the old boards of the back deck. The sound of my heart and my feet echoed in my ears. I had just walked away from the man that I loved, and it felt like a huge mistake. I needed a distraction. I needed to work.

The lobby was still deserted and silent. Where in the world was Brian? I went to the desk and checked behind it for any signs that he'd been there while I'd been on the beach, shooting my relationship dead.

Nothing.

Breakfast would be over at the diner by now and Brian should have been back already if that was where they had gone. So, where was he? And where were my parents?

There were guests arriving today and my mom had promised to make muffins for the guests, so we could offer treats and pastries like Grandma used to do. I walked to the dining room. Still deserted. I tried not to look through the windows and out at the beach beyond, but my eyes were drawn there anyway. Max tossed something into the water and Lucky jumped in after it. I wanted to join them, but the pain of his betrayal was still fresh and raw.

Besides, where had everyone gone? I listened intently at the bottom of the stairs. There was nothing coming from the rooms where we all slept. Uneasiness surfaced and I tried to dismiss it, but it wouldn't shrug off so easily.

Had some alien ship arrived in the middle of the night and hauled off my family? Had they decided to ditch work at the inn today and go out for an excursion? If so, why hadn't they woken me up or at least asked me to go with them?

I trudged up the stairs, and pressed my ear to Brian's door. Maybe he was napping. He could snore quite loudly, but I heard nothing. I put a hand on the doorknob and opened it. His bed was a mess, so it had been slept in, but otherwise there were no signs of life or my brother.

I frowned, closed the door, then went to Grandma's

master suite, which was the room my parents were using. I knocked several times, but got no answer. I knocked again. My knuckles hit the wood hard enough that they stung slightly, but there was still no answer.

Frustrated, I opened their door a crack and peeked in. Unlike Brian's room, theirs was neat as a pin, and their bed was made up. When I opened the door wider, I noticed a sheet of paper propped up against the pillows on the bed. What the . . .?

My knees almost gave out. I didn't want to read the note, but I had to know what it said. I took slow steps across the room, telling myself the entire time that it would just be a note saying they had gone to visit some wineries, or maybe to the farmer's market. But when I lifted the paper, and read the few words, my hopes vanished.

My parents were gone.

They had left me again.

This time they hadn't even had the guts to tell us they were leaving. Instead, they left this stupid note, written in Mom's loopy handwriting, propped up on the pillows of Grandma's bed.

I crumpled the paper in my fist, and threw it at the wall. Tears streamed down my face and I screamed as loud as I could, before clapping my hands to my mouth. All I needed was to have to explain myself to guests that I wasn't being attacked, but I may as well have been.

My parents were gone.

They'd left us.

Again.

Chapter Seventeen

I couldn't believe how few clothes I'd brought with me to Blue Moon Bay. How had I ever made do with such a short supply of things? I stared at the miniscule amount of jewelry on my bathroom counter, spotting the single Peridot earring, and my heart squeezed.

I remembered that first night out on the beach with Max. He'd noticed the one earring missing, and I could almost feel the touch of his fingers against my skin as he'd brushed my hair back behind my ear. It had only been hours since we'd ended things, and I already ached from missing him. I reminded myself that he'd let me down by keeping a huge secret from me.

He'd had his reasons, though. And he hadn't known that Grandma's will mandated that Brian and I had to sell the inn, or it would be donated to charity. He hadn't known, because I hadn't told him. I should've trusted him, and he should've trusted me, too. What a mess we'd made of something that had started out so perfect. I wanted to fix things between us, but I didn't know how to mend a relationship once it had been broken.

I looked down at the clothes strewn across my bed, waiting to go in the suitcase. Tears threatened, but I brushed them back. I couldn't stay in Blue Moon Bay after all. It wasn't old, painful memories driving me away this time. It was new fresh pain.

I slammed a dresser drawer shut and then kicked the closet door closed. I grabbed a heap of undergarments, and tossed them into the suitcase. More tears threatened, and this time I couldn't hold them back. Walking on the beach with Max had been a simple pleasure, but one that filled me with joy. When I'd worn Grandma's big hat, it had been like she was walking with us, and I knew she'd be proud of the responsible man that little balcony-jumping boy had become.

Of course Max couldn't blow off going to Tokyo. He'd made that promise to his dad before he'd met me, before he'd fallen in love with Blue Moon Bay. Max wasn't the kind of man who would go back on his word. I missed him so much in such a short time.

I had to get back to Sacramento, and get my life back on track. I had to put this whole mess behind me and start over again.

My suitcase looked ridiculously small, but it wasn't like I'd thrown much into the suitcase when I'd been so stunned and horrified from the news of Grandma's passing. It had only been a few weeks, but it felt like a lifetime ago. So much had happened.

My cell phone chimed, and my heart raced suddenly. Max! I grabbed my phone, and stared at the screen, but it wasn't Max. It was Janine.

I swiped the screen with my finger, and the message came up: *Good news that you're coming home. That other townhouse is still available. You're going to make your dreams come true after all.*

I sighed. The happiness I should've felt didn't come. I tapped out a reply, then set my phone back down, and reached for more clothes, but I didn't feel like packing anymore. Instead, I wandered over to the window, and gazed out at the lovely shining water below. How could a place so beautiful be so painful?

There was a knock at the door, and before I could say anything it opened. Brian appeared through the doorway, and he was holding a big guest book. He opened his mouth, but then his eyes shot to my suitcase, which lay open on the bed with all my stuff already in it.

"What's going on?" He came into the room, set the book on my nightstand, then looked up at me. "Why is your stuff in the suitcase? Didn't you ever unpack?"

I had to tell him the truth. I cleared my throat. "No, Brian. It's packed, because I'm leaving. I'm going back to Sacramento."

His green eyes pierced mine. "No, you can't go!"

"I know the thirty-day requirement period isn't up." I lifted my chin, and straightened my shoulders. "But what does it matter if this place goes to charity? Maybe then we can ensure it won't be torn down. Instead of letting Max's company do whatever he's planning to do with it."

"Max?" His face contorted, and he took a few steps toward me. When he spoke his voice shook and his shoulders did, too. "What does he have to do with anything?"

"He's the one who bought the inn. Apparently that's what he originally came to town to do. He claims he wanted to cancel the contract so we could keep it, but I told him the conditions of the will, and how we have to sell it."

He clenched his fingers together. "Have you lost your mind, Wendy? Did you drink some ocean water or something? You said you were going to stay in town."

I sighed. His eyes were glassy with tears, and mine were, too. I had to tell him the rest of it, and I didn't want to do that either. "Mom and Dad bailed. They lied to us, again. They up and left, leaving behind a stupid note. They didn't even have the guts to say goodbye in person this time."

His face went white, and he blinked a few times. Then he said, "Well, that figures. That's who they are, Wendy. They don't know anything besides leaving, but *you* don't have to leave."

I walked toward the suitcase. The long-sleeved shirt on the bed was the one I'd worn on my first sail with Max. Max, who had let me down just like my parents had. I grabbed the shirt, and tossed it in the suitcase. My vision blurred. "All I ever wanted was a family, but everyone leaves. You said it yourself a long time ago. People can't count on anyone but themselves. I've learned that now, just like you taught me when I was eight."

"I was wrong," he said, his voice barely a whisper. His green eyes widened, making him look like that scared, vulnerable boy in the diner all those years ago—the one whose parents had just left him. "When they told us they were leaving that day, it was like someone had reached inside me, and ripped out my heart. You turned to me for comfort and I was hurt, so I pushed you away. I'm so sorry," he said, the veins on his temples throbbing.

Tears burned my eyes. "Brian—"

"Can't you see how wrong I was?" His eyes filled, and I could see how much he was hurting. I wanted to put my arms around him, but he stepped toward me first. "Grandma *never* left us. Not for one single minute. She was here for us until the day she died."

Tears ran down my face, as I grabbed onto his arms, and nodded. "You're right. She never left us."

"You said all you ever wanted was family?" He choked on the last word, his face crumpling as he wrapped his hands around my arms. "You have *me*, sis. I let you down before, but I promise I never will again. I'll always be here for you. I'm sorry for pushing you away when we were young. I'm *so* sorry."

"I forgive you, Brian." After I said the words, long hard sobs started coming out of my mouth, and my whole body shook like I had some kind of plague. I didn't know who was more startled by that, Brian or me, but suddenly my big brother's arms were around me.

I had held all of that pain in for so long. Now that I'd forgiven, everything released in the huge sobs that followed. He rocked me back and forth, saying sweet big brother things like that he was here for me, and everything would be okay. So, I wept harder than I ever had in my entire life.

And it felt *good.* The pain and misery escaped me, rushing away until there was just this sort of clean numbness left behind. Brian hadn't meant to hurt me, and I hoped he'd never hurt me again. But I trusted that if he did, it wouldn't be intentional. I thought of Max and his secret, and something suddenly occurred to me.

I was pretty sure my nose was leaking horrible stuff, but I leaned back, swiping at my cheeks and nose, before I peered up at my big brother. "We can't sell Grandma's inn, Brian. We need to keep it safe and sound, the same way she kept us. I might know a way around the will."

Brian's phone rang, interrupting the moment. He glanced at the phone. "It's Mom."

I laughed at his strained look. He had good reason to worry about answering the phone, given how much emotion I'd just unleashed. "Answer it. I'm fine. I'm just going to unpack."

"We'll talk later." He hugged me again, as his phone rang, then he answered it with a quick hello as he headed out of my room.

I sighed, glanced out the window, then my gaze landed on the book on my nightstand. Confusion shot through me. Where had that come from? Oh, right. Brian had brought it in. I guessed it was the former guestbook, and I was right. There was also a smaller book lying on top of it, which looked like a journal.

I reached for the delicate book, opened a page, and the scent of lilacs drifted out to my nose, immediately invoking a memory of Grandma. A letter fell out, drifting down to the floor. I bent to pick it up, freezing in place when I recognized the handwriting as Grandma's too.

The letter was addressed to *me*.

****

The letter had a date, she had written it one month ago. I remembered she'd left Brian a letter, and it had never occurred to me that she'd leave one for me, too. I wanted to read the letter, but I was too scared. I'd let Grandma down, and so badly. I had left and never came back, and that had to have hurt her. But I'd been so blind to everything but my own hurt.

Anything Grandma said to me in that letter would be true. I had been wrong, so wrong, and it had taken me coming back here to see it. She had to have known that, and knowing Grandma—she had. She had probably set out to make me see how much I'd hurt Brian, so I could fix that. She had loved us, and I had loved her more than anyone I had ever known.

I held the letter and paced around my room. My suitcase was still on the bed, all my stuff still needed to be unpacked but I couldn't manage that right now. I didn't even care that there was a pair of bright pink panties sticking up from one side of the suitcase, waving around in the currents of air from the ceiling fan like some kind of crazy flag.

I went to the windows and gazed out at the ocean. From where I stood I could see the slice of beach that Max and I liked to walk on so much. I really wished that Max were here to calm me down and stand beside me as I read the letter. He would've held my hand, and told me that everything would be okay.

Only Max wasn't here. He was probably checked out and on his way to the airport, and then off to Japan, and he would be there for a long time. He'd be there so long I didn't know if he would still love me when he came back.

He would come back, though. He had said that Blue Moon Bay was his home, and I believed him. I believed *in* him, too. I should've trusted that he had good reasons for not telling me about the offer on the inn. I missed him terribly, and I wanted him back.

Letter in hand, I headed out of my room and the inn, and down to the beach. The water was calm, the waves lapping easily at the sand. I walked along the shore, staring out at the waves. The paper in my hand crackled in the slight wind, and I tightened my grip, but still didn't have the guts to read it. I stopped at the small monument at the bottom of the bluff, kicked off my shoes, and stared at the plaque that stood between the weathered pillars.

"Kissed by the Bay," I read, running my fingers along the bronze lettering. "One kiss, right here, under a blue moon will lead to love that lasts forever . . ."

I closed my eyes and could see my grandma, wearing a large hat over her perfectly coiffed hair, standing with her gardening tools in hand. A pang rolled through me. She had always given us everything she had to give: the run of the inn, the sea, her wisdom, and her love.

This was the same spot where she had told me about the legend for the first time. She had stood staring out at the sea, reciting the legend by heart, just loud enough to be heard over the waves. I had stared up at the big moon hanging over the ocean—the same blue moon that had hung in the sky the night I'd met Max.

After hearing the legend as a young girl, I'd hoped that one day I would be kissed right here by the man I was going to love forever. The page crackled again. I dug deep and found the courage to, finally, read the letter. I unfolded the page and looked at Grandma's handwriting again, that perfect script I had never been able to imitate.

My Dearest Wendy,

I know you're mad at me for making you come back and I don't blame you. I hope you know that my reasons and intentions are good, and that I did it because I needed you to learn something you couldn't discover in Sacramento.

I know that your parents have disappointed you, and if you give them the chance they will disappoint you again. But that doesn't mean everyone will.

Your parents are people who can't stay in one place. It isn't in them. I wish it were different, and that we'd all been able to spend more time together. I can't blame your mom, either, because the truth is your dad was always a wanderer and as restless as the waves on the beach.

When he met your mom I knew I had lost him, but I also knew I had lost him to a woman who would always hold him as the dearest thing she had ever known. They are two sides of the same coin, and while I wish they were different for you, at the same time I'm glad they aren't. Because they found the love that most people only ever dream of, and they have kept it alive. Lasting love is special and rare, even if it's not always convenient or kind to people outside of it.

You're not like your parents, Wendy. You enjoy seeing new places, but you don't have that inborn need to leave. You were never looking past the horizon or wondering what is over the next hill or on the other side of the ocean.

You're not like them at all. I know you might think you are because you left Blue Moon Bay, but you weren't running toward something, you were running from the hurt. I forced your return, which I don't doubt you did on Brian's behalf. You have a choice now. You can choose to be alone, to protect yourself like I did, thinking that every man will disappoint you. Or you can accept people for who they are and adjust your expectations on what they can give you. Whatever you decide, don't view their faults as a measure of their love for you.

Let me tell you a story. I know you already know the legend of Blue Moon Bay, but I want to tell it again so bear with me.

One kiss, right here, under a blue moon will lead to love that lasts forever. . . .

Know the history of two young people, the daughter

of locals and the son of summer guests, who fell helplessly in love at this very beach. When their parents discovered their relationship, they were forbidden to see each other. His parents felt the working girl was beneath their son and her parents feared the scandal could ruin their business. But the night before the family was to return home, the son got a note to his sweetheart and they met here under the stars.

He pleaded with her to wait a year for him to turn eighteen and become a man—that until then they could write to each other in secret and he'd find a way for them to be together. The young girl knew their parents would never allow that to happen, though. She'd always obeyed her parents and wasn't strong enough to go against their wishes, even for the perfect love she shared with him.

So, with broken hearts, they said goodbye to each other right here at this very spot. A blue moon hung in the night sky, illuminating their final kiss and they promised to love each other always. Then they vowed that everyone who kissed at this exact point by the bay, under a blue moon, would be in love forever—and would never separate as they tragically had.

That woman in the story was me. Your dad never knew his father, but he was my one and only love. He wanted us to stay together long distance but I didn't think that would work out so I cut things off altogether. He didn't give up on our love, I did, by not being willing to stand strong for what I believed in. After all of this time, I still think of him and wonder, "What if. . .?"

While I can't go back in time, I can give you the wisdom of my experience. Don't close your heart. And don't close your mind. You just need the courage to recognize love for what it is, even if it looks different from what you expect.

You're like me in many ways. Not all of them good. I withdrew from people, thinking I was protecting my heart, but all of that safety has a price. Safety, all too often, leaves you alone. You remind me of myself when I was young, wanting love so badly but thinking it needs to fit a certain mold. In truth, some of the best love comes from the opposite of how we think life should go. Love comes in different forms, sometimes unexpectedly, like when a grandmother finds herself burdened with raising her young grandkids, then discovers it was her life's greatest joy.

Yours,

Grandma

Tears spilled down my cheeks, one after the other. I had always thought Grandma had been mad at Mom and Dad for dumping two kids off on her. I had always felt abandoned but I hadn't been. I'd been lodged into a safe harbor, by two people who were always pulling up the anchor.

I couldn't believe my grandma was the woman in the legend. She had spent her entire lifetime wondering if she had made the wrong choice. She had been afraid to fight harder, just like me, and she had lost the man who would have been hers forever.

"Oh, Grandma. I'm so sorry I left, and that I didn't come back." I dropped to my knees, fingering the warm sand, as a sprinkling of saltwater sprayed my face, and mingled with my tears. "I never saw that I had a home and family right here with you. I hope you forgive me, and know how much I loved you. I'm glad you brought me back here, too. This is where I belong, and this is where I'm going to stay forever."

I had to find Max and tell him I was wrong—that I was willing to fight hard for us, and never let him go. He was probably already at the airport. I had to hurry!

Chapter Eighteen

Adrenaline pumped through my veins as I jumped to my feet. I needed to get to the airport before Max took off. I had to tell him that I loved him, and that I had been scared—too scared—to even try, but I was ready now.

Max wasn't leaving *me*. He was not pulling up the anchor and heading for a far horizon. He was going to work, and coming home again. He was not a dreamer or a drifter, any more than I was. I grabbed my shoes and held them in my hand as I dashed for the stairs so fast that little puffs of sand spurted up around my feet and ankles. Just as I got to the bottom of the steps, Lucky came galloping down, her golden hair flying, and her mouth stretched.

And behind her was Max.

He was peering down at me, his blue eyes stormy, and I stopped in my tracks. My hand gripped the wooden railing for support, then I started up again. I hurried past Lucky's licks, giving her a quick pat, then I stopped on the step above him so we were eye to eye.

"I can't believe you're here." I wanted to throw my arms around him, but twiddled my fingers instead, hoping he wanted to hear what I had to say. "I was just coming to the airport to tell you I'm sorry. When you get back from Japan, I'll be right here, waiting for you, no matter how long you're gone. We can email, call each other, do video chat, or whatever else we have to do. That is, if you still want to. I was just scared, but I'm not anymore. Can you forgive me? And what are you doing here?"

He bent his head, giving me an intense look that reached my soul. "I thought I had blown it, too. I should've talked to you about my reason for being in town, but I was afraid of messing things up. Looks like I managed to do that, anyway. I need to go on this business trip, but I couldn't go without giving you the present I'd found for you."

I blinked. "What?"

He handed me a small box. "Open it."

My fingers shook as I lifted the lid. Lucky bumped my legs and then licked my hand, whining softly as she did so. I patted her head, then opened the tiny box, which revealed a small Peridot earring. I gasped, putting my hand to my mouth. "Oh, Max. You didn't have to replace this. I could've lost the earring in the ocean when my hysterical twin appeared."

He chuckled. "I got it for you the very next day, but I was afraid of scaring you off if I gave it to you too soon." He smiled, then handed me a long rectangular box. "Since you seem all right with the earring, this is for you as well."

"Another gift?" I bit my lip as I lifted the top off the second box. Inside lay a gorgeous pendant on a platinum chain. It was a perfectly round blue opal, with splashes of green that matched the gems in my earrings. I smiled up at him, knowing exactly what this pendant was supposed to represent. "Is this a full moon?"

He nodded. "The second full moon of the month, which makes it a blue moon." He clasped the necklace around me, then planted a light kiss to the back of my neck, sending a rush of tingles down my spine. "The perfect time to kiss the girl I want to be with forever."

"I feel the same way about you." I slipped my arms around his neck, staring up into his beautiful blue eyes. He peered down at me with a look of longing and love.

No more words were needed. He pressed his mouth to mine, which said it all. It was the kiss of a lifetime, on the steps that led to the spot by the bay where dreams were promised to come true, and people were guaranteed to fall in love forever. I could hear the waves breaking, and feel the steady throb of Max's heart against my chest.

When we came up for air, I kept my arms around his neck. "If you'd still like me to have the inn, I'd like to buy it back from you after escrow closes. We have to sell the inn, per the will's instructions, but there are no restrictions on us buying it back."

"Clever thinking." He chuckled, his breath warm against my cheek. "I'll sell it back to you with one request. I'd like to keep the abandoned restaurant. I'm sorry I never told you the details about my business. I own a restaurant group, but we usually lease the properties. My dad wanted to purchase the inn, and let me lease from him to combine our companies. He was not happy when I refused to sign that contract."

"A restaurant, huh?" I pressed my lips to the corner of his mouth, loving the feel of my mouth on his skin. Keeping my kiss there, I asked, "Will I get a discount on my meals?"

He smiled, then captured my mouth with his in a long, warm, kiss. "That is definitely negotiable."

I sighed in his arms. "My grandma would have loved you."

"I think she did love me when she saw the awesome job I did on her hedges." He held me in his arms, and stared out at the weathered pillars below. "It wouldn't shock me at all if she's the one who sent me back here at the same time she conned you into coming home."

"It wouldn't surprise me, either. My grandma always had some kind of plan up her sleeve." I laughed, before kissing him again and again.

****

The Pumpkin Festival was in full swing. Local pop and rock bands played on a little stage, and while some people grumbled about new changes, most were ecstatic to see them there. The dunking booth was in working order and I recognized one of my high school teachers sitting in the booth, his feet dangling into the water while he heckled the crowd in a good natured way to get them to try their luck at sending him into the cold ocean water.

Per his word, Brian dressed like a clown, and wandered around the festival giving out giant cones of pastel pink cotton candy to the kids. "Great job, Olivia. This is the biggest turnout I've ever seen."

Olivia looked pretty in a yellow sundress. "It was a lot of work, but well worth it. I can't believe you let Megan talk you into being a clown. The kids love it."

"Everyone loves a good clown," Megan said, stealing a piece of Brian's cotton candy.

Max pointed to a suspiciously creaky mini roller coaster. "We have got to ride that."

"I hope your life insurance is paid up in full," Brian joked. "I saw them putting it together and trust me, there were some parts left over. That can't be a good sign."

I elbowed my brother, and cuddled up to Max. "Ignore him. He's a big scaredy cat, and always has been. We can't ever get him on a roller coaster."

"It's because I have good sense." Brian dabbed a piece of cotton candy against Megan's nose.

"I'm with you, Brian." She giggled, snatching more cotton candy, and eating it. "Oh, Wendy! I have the mock-up ready for that billboard design you wanted for the inn. Should I come by tomorrow and show it to you?"

"Sounds great." I nodded, grabbing a piece of cotton candy, too. The billboard would hang right by the highway and with Megan's creativity on full display it was sure to attract new guests.

I headed for the game next to the house of mirrors, while Max stopped to play a game beside that one. Just as I was about to decide to plunk my money down and play, my phone rang and I paused to see who was calling me.

It was Janine, so I answered, "Hi, Janine."

"Guess who just got their real estate license?" she blurted.

I grinned. "You."

"Yes! I passed that test with a great score, thanks to you. So when are you going to start your own company down there so I can come and work for you?"

I chuckled. "One day, maybe soon. Right now I'm still trying to get my inn and family back on its feet. Priorities, you know."

"Well, efficiency is one of your strong suits, so I'm sure I won't be slaving away up here forever. Oh, and guess what?"

"What?"

"The people who bought your dream townhome claim it's haunted and has a bad foundation. You dodged a bullet there."

I laughed and said goodbye, but then my phone rang again. I glanced at the screen, thinking it was Janine again. But, nope. It was my mom. I stood there, staring at my phone, and then I answered it. I sucked in a breath. "Hello?"

"Wendy?" Mom's voice cracked, and she sounded close to tears. "I-I was just going to leave a message. I didn't think you were going to answer."

"I love you, Mom," I said, and what I also meant by that was that I forgave her.

She hiccupped into the receiver. "Oh, Wendy. I'm sorry to disappoint you again. I wanted to stay because you needed us, but I felt suffocated in Blue Moon Bay. I don't know why. It's not your father's fault . . ."

She loved him enough to take all the blame, even if it meant that I was mad at her. I thought of Grandma's letter, and her saying that Dad was always looking past the horizon long before Mom came into his life. Grandma hadn't wanted to lose him, but she had set him free to find his own way. She'd chosen to let them be happy no matter what that meant for her.

I decided she'd been trying to set us free when she forced us to sell the inn. I was sure she thought she was setting Brian and me free, but she didn't realize how much we loved the inn. Probably because we'd never told her. Sigh.

"Where are you two?" I asked.

"In a mountain cabin near Tahoe. We're thinking of staying here awhile."

I wanted to laugh. That could mean anything with those two. It could mean a week, or a year. Who knew where the wind would blow them? But that was who they were and I accepted that now. "Mom, it's okay. I understand. And maybe we can all come up and visit you at Thanksgiving."

She took a long audible breath. "I'd love that, Wendy. I really would."

"Me too," I said, and meant it. Nine years was a long time to ignore someone, and it was time to stop that. Maybe she and Dad would never be the traditional parents that I had always wanted, but they were my parents, flaws and all.

"I love you, Wendy. Give Brian my love, too."

"I will." I spotted Max coming toward me with a big cheesy grin on his face and his hands behind his back. "I have to go, but we'll talk soon. Call me any time you want, Mom. I'm not going to ignore you anymore. I promise."

"I'm not going to ignore you, either. Not ever."

We said goodbye and hung up. Max walked up and smiled mischievously. "Look what I won in the dart game for you. I hit three balloons in a row."

He pulled his hands from behind his back, and held out a glass whale filled with clear blue liquid. Tingles prickled up my arms. I stared at the glass whale in awe. This was the prize I'd always wanted to win at the Pumpkin Festival, and now Max had given it to me. I wanted to tell my grandma, but I had a strong feeling she already knew. In a way, I felt this was a sign from her, to tell me she knew I'd healed my old wounds, and that she was happy for me.

"I love it." I lifted up on my tiptoes to give Max a

long, slow kiss.

"I love you," he breathed, then he took my hand and led me toward the ride that Brian and Megan were afraid to go on. He turned to me. "Do you like roller coasters?"

"I'm game if you are." I lifted my brows. In answer, he slipped his arm around my waist and led me to the roller coaster, where we rode up and down at high speed, until it felt like my stomach would fall out. But through our laughs and screams, we survived. We stepped off the ride, planted our feet on firm ground again, and our friends surrounded us.

A feeling of peace washed through me. I glanced out at the bay, the sun glinting off the waves in diamond-shaped flashes of light. I hadn't wanted to return to Blue Moon Bay, but in the end—just like always—Grandma had been right. Finally, I was home.

My life may not have gone the way I'd planned, but that didn't mean it hadn't gone according to a *greater* plan. I'd dreamed of the legend as a child . . . that being kissed at that special spot by the bay, under the blue moon, would lead to love that lasted forever. Somewhere along the way I'd lost hope, but deep down I'd always believed.

The feelings Max and I had for each other were built on genuine emotion and trust. We'd have to work hard to nurture our relationship every day of our lives. Yet, I'd always cherish the knowledge that our love was strengthened by fate from that sacred kiss we shared the first night we met. Together, we'd made the Kissed by the Bay legend come true.

The End

SUSAN HATLER is a *New York Times* and *USA Today* Bestselling Author, who writes humorous and emotional contemporary romance and young adult novels. Many of Susan's books have been translated into German, Spanish, French, and Italian. A natural optimist, she believes life is amazing, people are fascinating, and imagination is endless. She loves spending time with her characters and hopes you do, too.

You can reach Susan here:

Facebook: facebook.com/authorsusanhatler
Twitter: twitter.com/susanhatler
Website: susanhatler.com
Blog: susanhatler.com/category/susans-blog

Ellen signs up for online dating because lasting love is all about compatibility . . .

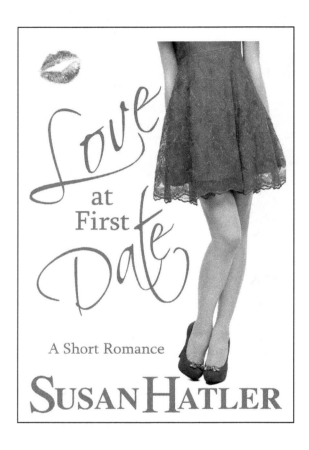

Love
at
First
Date

A Short Romance

SUSAN HATLER

. . . so why can't she stop
thinking about Henry when he's
the opposite of everything she wants?

Truth or Dare is all fun and games . . .

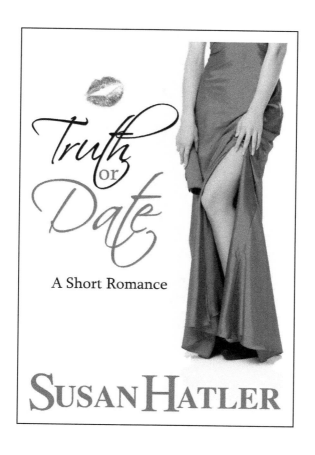

Truth or Date

A Short Romance

SUSAN HATLER

. . . until a spontaneous dare has Gina
falling for the office playboy.

It's Valentine's Day and Rachel can stay home and watch
TV . . .

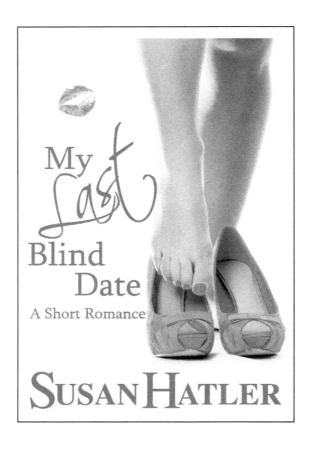

My *Last*
Blind
Date

A Short Romance

SUSAN HATLER

. . . or risk another dating disaster
by trying yet again for love.

Kristen swears off men, but temptation
swoops in . . .

Save
the
Date

A Short Romance

SUSAN HATLER

. . . when her sexy friend Ethan
starts flirting with her.

Will Melanie have to follow her
best friend's narrow dating rules . . .

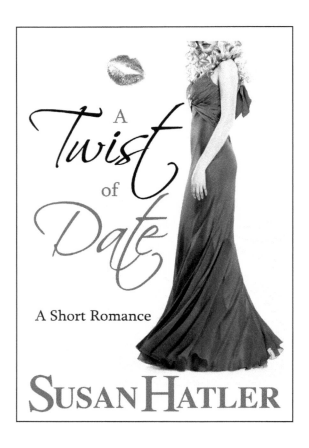

A
Twist
of
Date

A Short Romance

SUSAN HATLER

. . . in order to find lasting love?

Kaitlin agrees to five dates in five days . . .

License
to
Date

A Short Romance

SUSAN HATLER

. . . only to fall for the mysterious bartender
who's there to witness them all.

When Jill's promotion is nabbed by nepotism, she
is offered another position on the partner-track . . .

Driven
to
Date

A *Special* Edition

SUSAN HATLER

. . . by pretending to date Ryan—
the man who got her job.

Ginger donates her decorating services
to a charity auction . . .

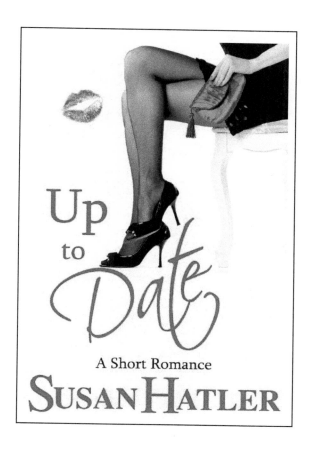

Up
to
Date

A Short Romance

SUSAN HATLER

. . . and now must work for the one man
with the power to break her heart.

In high school, it's tough enough reading Steinbeck and
Shakespeare . . .

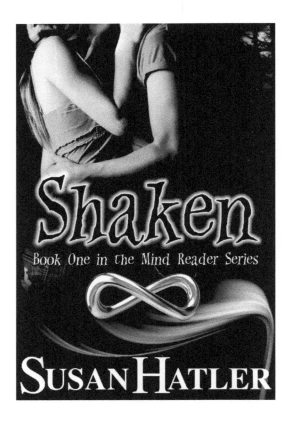

. . . now Kylie has to read minds.

CPSIA information can be obtained
at www.ICGtesting.com
Printed in the USA
LVHW08s2046170718
584087LV00005B/819/P